The Colour Black

First published in this edition in Great Britain 2014 by
Jacaranda Books Art Music Ltd
98b Sumatra Road,
West Hampstead
London NW6 1PP
www.jacarandabooksartmusic.co.uk

A CIP catalogue record for this book is available from the British Library

ISBN: 978 1 90976 202 2

Edited, designed and typeset by Head & Heart Publishing Services
www.headandheartpublishingservices.com

Printed and bound in Great Britain by Gomer, Llandysul, Wales

The Colour Black

Maia Walczak

JACARANDA

To all beings. And to 'Being' itself.

For when you look through a prism,
The light is refracted.
You don't see what's in front of you.
Your mind is distracted.

the day I woke up

writing the letter

Jack's valley

that beautiful stormy night

finding Oak

crossing the border

the magic island

first swim

dancing

The Colour Black

Black is the absence of light.
Yet it is also the complete absorption of it.
Therefore, black can be both void of light and totally full of it.
Most days I am void of light, but I've had rare moments
when it has taken over me completely. - Silvia Cruz

Reality and Perception

When I was little I looked at the sea and I saw eternity. I looked at my hand and I was staring at infinity. The world was a divine dance, and the eyes through which I saw it were also infinite. The sea a dancing shimmering jewel that sung the most incredible song. The world a delicious magic trick to behold, and I, the little girl standing on the shore, knew that life was a gift in which I could marvel at this magic endlessly. An unknown and mysterious benefactor had bestowed this gift unto me. And yet, somehow, the giver, the receiver and the gift were inseparable. They were all one. For there were no divisions. No boundaries. I had all the time in the world to enjoy this weird and wonderful gift. For even though I hadn't yet quite learned the trapping concept of time, I felt that no matter how much time there was before I died, there was enough – more than enough to enjoy this miracle. The colours, the sounds, the movement, the light, the wind, the warmth… all the infinite whispering song of the universe. What a gift to have so much time to enjoy something that didn't even require time to make it enough. When I was a child, standing on the shore, I needed nothing more. I was complete. It was all complete. I had seen the miracle, and that was enough.

I looked up at my mami standing by my side. She was frowning.

I knew she was wrong. Couldn't she see? Couldn't she see the turquoise, emeralds and jades singing to us and embracing us with their love? Couldn't she feel it too? She bent down and put her arm around me. It wasn't the same love I felt from the cliffs, the sand, the sky and the sea. It was different, but it was my mami's love – beautiful, warm, safe.

'Hurry Silvia,' she said, 'we have to go.'

My mami's eyes and mine were open and looking. But she wasn't stunned by the life that was pulsating, vibrating, before us. She wasn't mesmerised by the colours. She wasn't taken aback by the miracle of existence. She was numb to it. This divine magic trick was staring at her, and all she could say was 'hurry up'. Her eyes only saw the sea. It was just the sea. That's all she had to know. She had learnt the word for it. She had learnt all the labels for everything in the world, so she no longer had to truly see any of it.

'We need to go.'

She picked me up and she ran.

*

We see life through a prism. We are animals. Our instinct is to survive. We must eat, drink, sleep, and protect ourselves from prey. We avoid death. We seek pleasure and run from pain. My mami knew she had to run, so she ran. Those guards were angry, very angry – they wouldn't have hesitated with their guns. It wasn't the first time Mami had snuck into some forbidden place to take photos during her journalism days. They probably already knew who she was, and if they didn't, they would soon find out. She was easily recognisable and didn't bother much with disguises.

Imagine if I had suddenly been able to make those men with their guns see what I could see and feel through my four-year-old eyes. They'd never threaten or kill anyone again. Why would they? They'd be too busy savouring the beauty and wonder of the universe and existence. Too busy enjoying this inexplicable gift. Had it been possible to suddenly shock them with the vision of this wonderful world, we'd never have had to run.

But what could I have said? What words could I have used? What could I have told them to make them see? To see the world for what it is, and not for what we are. To see the world clearly, without concepts. To experience life directly, without prisms. How can anyone possibly change the perception of another?

Luckily, that day on the beach, Mami picked me up and she ran.

Jet Black and Poppy Red

Twenty years on, I lay half naked on the cold marble floor, staring up at the ceiling. It was so cold. Maybe if I could stand physical coldness like this I'd be able to confront any cold reality. Coldness would become normal. Acceptable. Permissible. The joint was reaching its end. My hand moved slowly to my mouth and I inhaled one last time before placing the butt on the floor. I got up too quickly and the head rush blinded me for a few seconds.

It was time for a post-Sunday-joint treat: peanut butter, banana and chocolate sandwich with a cold vanilla shake to be enjoyed in front of the TV. Stupid TV. Mindless. But somehow far more mesmerising after two joints. The moving images and sounds became hypnotic, the tastes, textures and smell of the food so pleasurable. Why couldn't this be a constant state? Today nothing mattered. Sunday: the day of rest. The day of forgetting everything. Almost forgetting.

I licked chocolate spread off my fingers, got up off the sofa and went back for seconds. I made another sandwich. Neat. Clean. I placed it on a small white plate and set it down on the marble worktop. Clink. I turned around to look out of the panoramic windows: walls of glass that looked out at the city. San Diego looked hazy today. There was less contrast in the summer sky, the buildings and the mountains. The sun was shining, but everything looked faded. I placed both hands against the vast cold glass, pressed my cheek to it. Far below, the city was alive and moving as always. The cars, the people, the rush. If I could just step through and out from behind this solid invisible object and fly out over the city, far into the mountains. If I could just fly. Fly wherever. I looked back down at the streets below. What would it be like to fall all that way? I had a sudden spasm of vertigo and pulled back from the window. I turned back around to look at the room. The kitchen, the diner, the living room: all mine. All one huge cold space bordered by these glass walls that looked out onto the world. The sky that made me long to fly. And as I stood there, I had a rare moment of peace. Taking in this cold heartless lie of a home, I suddenly felt a temporary peace.

I turned on the stereo and with a slow sadness I danced around to an indulgently melancholic playlist. Round and round like a ghost. Barely there. Before I knew it, it was dark outside. More television. A film. And then goodnight. Sundays were all about this. Pottering about. Achieving nothing. Going nowhere. Seeing no one. Sleep. The dreamworld. Disappearing behind my closed eyes into nothingness. Oblivion. Ceasing to exist for a while. My comfort zone.

*

Monday. Good morning. Go on, knock 'em dead Silvia. Show the world you mean business. I pouted in front of the bathroom mirror. Red lipstick; a little joke I played with myself and on the world. I flipped the tube over and read the base: 'Poppy Red'. I could remember beautiful fields of opium poppies from my childhood. My memories were nothing to smile about but I breathed in and grinned at the mirror. Now was not the time to think about any of that. If I wore nothing else, I had to wear the red lipstick. Walking through the city streets, would it dazzle them? Would I stand out? Would they think, *wow, she's special?* I didn't know, but I would have liked them to. I wanted to be the muse for a change. I ran my fingers through my long black hair, detangling it all the way down to my waist, and I stared into my blue eyes. *Bluer than the ocean,* my mother would say. I picked up the black eyeliner and ran a long line of it above each eye. At least you knew what you were getting with poppy red lipstick and jet-black eyeliner. Real red. Proper black.

I turned on the tap and scrubbed behind my nails. My hands were getting grubby and dry with all the chalk and charcoal these days. I rubbed moisturiser into them, paying particular attention to the long scar on my right hand. It ran from the underside of my thumb to just above my wrist. The scar. Another reminder. I strutted to the supermarket, past the flower stall, where the scent of oriental lilies and freesias was especially intense today, past the Jewish bakery, its deliciously sweet aroma making my mouth water, past the cinema, and past the same homeless guy who always stared at me as if he knew me. I stopped to look up at the sky for a brief moment, the tall buildings looming over me. I closed my eyes for a second as I breathed it all in. *Hurry up. It's Monday. There are things to get done.* Must get supplies from the shop and then get back, eat, and prepare materials for today's sessions. Max was coming at noon. Ah. Max. And who was after him? I checked my diary. Arthur.

Today would be a success. I could feel it. Today I felt a huge drive to create. I suddenly felt impatient. I felt I could rush home, get a huge slab of paper and create a masterpiece. To feel inspiration when you're nowhere near the drawing board is easy enough. When you're finally there with the charcoal in your hand, sometimes you feel like you're forcing yourself to do the work.

But other times you're lucky, and the most beautiful wave of inspiration hits when you're sitting in front of the blank piece of paper. You can sit there for hours in a state of total flow, disconnected from the world you usually inhabit – the world of worries, unnecessary thoughts and emotions. Time does not exist and the only thing is this moment. Here. The paper, the markings, my hand, the charcoal, the process. I am not drawing. Drawing is happening. And the world as I usually know it no longer seems real at all. Sometimes I feel like I live for those moments. Sometimes I feel like they are trying to tell me something.

I was looking forward to drawing both Arthur and Max today. Their bodies inspired me – both in their own separate ways. But there'd be no sex today, I was feeling far too vulnerable. I couldn't be bothered with that game today.

The Meaning of Meaning

Max was early as usual, which annoyed me. It made me feel rushed, and that pissed me off. He was a personal trainer with far too much time on his hands. But it was always the same when I greeted him at the door, I found him so physically attractive that it often left me feeling stupid. I don't even know why I bothered drawing him. I really don't know. We found each other such a turn on, his naked body showing clear signs of it every time I tried to draw him, that it just meant I spent more time in bed with him than using him as a model. So what the fuck was I paying him for? When I brought it up he said the only solution was to meet up outside of work hours. But no. I wasn't going there. I had no interest in forming any sort of relationship with him, sexual or otherwise. There was no attraction there except for a physical one, and the sex simply wasn't enough to draw me to him in any other way. The sex just happened because it had to. It was like scratching an itch. That's all it was. I didn't have to make a ritual out of it. Besides, he had already started prying into my past, so spending any more time with him would quite clearly only make that worse.

I had on many occasions contemplated firing him, but though I hated to admit it, the scratching of the itch had become addictive. Plus a series based on my drawings of him had sold pretty well after a critic had called it a 'new and interesting line of sexual and carnal pieces, taking the artist deeper into her primal self'.

When I say critic, I should perhaps mention here that I was a very little known artist. This critic was in fact just a part-time art blogger who'd followed my work for a while, and supposed he knew something about me. About my 'soul'. He tended to write similar types of things about other artists too, stuff that, in my opinion, sounded like the pretentious ramblings of a newly graduated History of Art student.

But oh god, how could I have resisted Max's body? I hated myself for it, yet sometimes I felt relieved to have these simple moments that reminded me I was just another human being with instinctive impulses towards physical pleasure. It was so uncomplicated, innocent and untainted by thought. I was over-analysing it all again. I just wished I wasn't paying money to create unfinished drawings. Perhaps unfinished drawings would be my next big thing. I was sure I could find a critic who'd come up with a suitably pretentious thing to say about that.

Here he was again at my door. No body contact at greeting, that was always the way. Over the last few days I'd actually allowed myself to think about things a little more than usual. All sorts of things. I'd allowed myself to delve a little deeper. Maybe I was just getting tired of always resisting certain thoughts. Of course I didn't delve too deep, because there were certain thoughts I feared would lead me to a place that was far too painful for me to handle at that moment. In any case, my recent introspection meant that today I despised him a bit more than usual.

In the two hours since he'd rung the doorbell I'd managed to finish two large and fairly elaborate sketches, which I was happy with. Not once did I hesitate, I was so engrossed in drawing that I didn't even feel turned on. It was wonderful. Today held one of those rare moments where I had become totally involved in what I was doing. It had been such a long time since I had felt like this.

Max didn't say much, thankfully. Perhaps he felt that I was clearly uninterested in him sexually today. Maybe I came across rude. But in any case his silence made it all the more easy. What a breath of fresh air. I had enjoyed his body in a totally different way today.

At exactly 2pm I put the charcoal down. I walked towards the panoramic windows and looked out at the wide San Diego skyline. For a moment I was completely oblivious to the fact I had someone in my presence. I looked out at the world, mesmerised. Feeling the effects of my creative high. It was like a drug. Max cleared his throat. I looked his way to acknowledge him and started wiping my hands clean with a piece of kitchen roll. I watched it darken as it took away the black dust from my hands. He made some other little noise to once again remind me he was there. I looked up at him and surprised myself by smiling at him. And then I looked again at the world outside.

'What do you see when you look out of here?' I said.

'Huh?'

I repeated the question.

'I swear you've asked me this before,' he said, 'well… obviously there's buildings and stuff.'

'No, but what do you see? What do you really see?'

I wanted him to describe the colours, tell me they were rich, dull, vibrant, whatever. I wanted to know.

'Huh?'

'Nothing. It doesn't matter.'

I moved towards the kitchen and asked him if he wanted anything. He sniggered.

'Just the usual,' he said.

I knew what he meant by that and I'd expected such a response. And with no thought, no ounce of wondering or analysing, my mind still at peace and still on a high from the full two hours of flow, I approached him smiling, stupidly, like he never usually saw me smile, and we did it right there on the sheet where he had been posing for me.

But an hour and a half later, as I was closing the door behind him, my high was replaced by a sinking feeling, like I was shrinking back to my usual constrained and restricted me. The me that I lived with on a daily basis. Heavy and solid – so different to the 'me' that existed in my moments of flow. In those moments I didn't feel small and limited, I felt boundless. But the bliss was now gone and I had retracted back to the little me. The joy of simply *being* was replaced by the weight of *being somebody*: this adult called Silvia, who could never be content.

I ate a late lunch at the kitchen table, staring into the void of the room. The more I stared, the more sadness I felt. I got up and turned up the radio, on the most commercial channel, and I shook away the feeling. I danced like an idiot for a minute and then did twenty star jumps whilst forcing myself to smile. These were the crazy rituals you could have when living alone. You didn't have to act level-headed or composed, you were allowed to oscillate between emotional extremes. There was no one to judge how insane all this looked. After that I went and cut myself a sizeable piece of carrot cake and brewed the perfect cup of milky tea. I sat back down at the kitchen table, smiled at the snacks. Delicious. Sweet, spicy, creamy, perfect. I reminded myself that I, too, was allowed to be a normal and light-hearted person. Even if things got me down, it was okay, that was just life, a part of life, it wasn't me, it wasn't who I was. Sadness was something that just happened sometimes. I didn't have to take it all too seriously.

Cake and tea. How normal and lovely and nice. I was now all set for an afternoon of drawing Arthur. Arthur was a mature art student. I had actually once agreed to pose for him too, but only the once. After I'd slept with him for the first time I could tell he was slightly more sensitive than some of the other men I'd dealt with. That's why I'd refused to sleep with him again for a long time after that. But the sexual tension grew too strong, so I had to make it clear: it was only sex. And it could all stop at any moment. Those were my terms. That was my disclaimer to them all.

And an afternoon of drawing – not quite in the state of flow as before – and sex ensued. Sex with Arthur was never a given, but today it happened. He was much more affectionate than the others, which I loved, but sometimes felt a little guilty about.

It was rare for me to get two drawing sessions with two different men on the same day. It felt strange having had sex with both of them only a few hours apart. Sometimes I caught myself wondering how I really felt about all these reckless flings I was having. But nobody was getting hurt, and I enjoyed it, whether it meant anything or not. And what is meaning? Isn't it just an afterthought we add onto experiences, to try and make sense of our lives? So that life doesn't end up feeling as pointless as it actually is? I enjoyed those intimate moments while they lasted, and that was meaningful enough for me.

But, that evening, when I was alone again, I sat down against the cold metal of the radiator and I cried. I had never cried about any of it before. Why was I suddenly feeling so strange about what I was doing with these men? Was I looking for something more seemingly meaningful? God no. That too was all a load of bullshit. I had long ago learnt enough about all that. All that romantic love shit was just an ego thing – people's insecurity searching for gratification in someone else. Whatever. I didn't need that. I didn't even fucking want that. And, most of all, I couldn't have that.

I decided to blame this sudden outburst of emotions on the new pill I was taking. Fucking hormones. I'd started taking it a couple of months ago, after I'd skipped a period, found out I was pregnant and had to go through an abortion. Imagine me bringing a child into this world, now that would be really tragic.

I ran a bath and lay in it for almost an hour, until the water cooled, staring into space. Sometimes, quite often, I liked to submerge myself under the water completely, slowly sinking my head further and further down, keeping my eyes open. It was like disappearing from the world for a moment. A moment of relief. A momentary escape. I was but the blur of a body against a blur of white bath. I listened to the high-pitched ringing in my ears. I breathed out bubbles and watched them rise. Underwater. Submerged. Like a foetus. Sometimes I'd be under there a little too long. Testing… Then I'd rise up, gasping for air.

The rest of my week would be quite different. For the next two days I'd be completely alone. I had no one booked in, so I would just work on my large-scale abstract pieces – for it was mostly when I worked on them that I encountered those incredible moments of flow. They allowed me to create whatever I wanted without premeditation, without planning. With them my hands and mind were free.

On Thursday Pete was coming over. He was my plumper client. I'd chosen him because of that. There was no point having all these different men unless they all had different bodies to draw – some tall, some small, some ripped like a marble statue, some fatter than Santa. Pete was in his late fifties, married, and a slightly eccentric hippy. It seemed as though he spent half his time laughing. It was always easy to be around him. He arrived on time, was kind, respectful and left on time. I was always happy with the drawings that came out of our sessions. He was money very well spent. I knew more about him than any of the others, simply because he chatted so much when posing for me. He had once mentioned something about having worked as an immigration lawyer or something like that, but mostly he talked about his personal life. His wife, he'd talk so much about his wife. But, above all, I liked him because he didn't ask many questions about me. He'd sensed I didn't like it.

After Pete I would be alone again until next week, when my diary showed that I had a different man coming on each day. Weeks like that were rare too. But then again, I never really had a regular structure. Two of the men coming the next week were men I'd sleep with on occasion.

I actively avoided attachment, or that thing people called 'love relationships'. I had seen what it had done to my mother, and even as a little girl I vowed to myself that I would learn from her mistakes. I told myself that if I ever should falter and start wondering whether this 'love' thing was actually good, all I had to do was think back to when I was a young girl observing my mother's bad choices. That couldn't be me. I simply couldn't allow myself to be that person – blinded.

Perhaps all my issues wouldn't be so bad if I had someone to talk to. But when you're sworn to secrecy how can you talk, even if you wanted to? Who could I possibly ever talk to? It was impossible. It just wasn't safe. I had to keep it inside.

The idea of 'normality' was like paradise to me: distant, deceptive and unattainable. I was born never to know the more normal human experience of the people who surrounded me: the people who waited in line with me in the supermarket, the people I painted, the people who rushed around in the city below. If only they realised just how lucky they were.

The Man With No Name

I woke up feeling great. The sun was streaming onto the bed cocooning me in its warmth, the sky was without a hint of cloud and I, sitting up on the mattress, felt like a normal person. I felt less guarded and less like I had things to hide. On days like these I liked to brunch at the café to celebrate this feeling, to drag it out.

I headed to Lenny's, one of the nicer cafés in the local area. Maybe I could make eye contact with a good-looking waiter or a man sat across at another table. Today it would be the latter: a muscular guy, with dark skin and dark hair, but with the most alluring light eyes. Once we'd made eye contact for the third time I started to wonder if I was making him feel uncomfortable. Before I had chance to ponder it further, he gave me a flirtatious smile. But, before I had chance to smile back, someone had sat down at my table and stolen my attention. It was that homeless man, the one who always seemed to stare. Except now he really was staring at me. He tried a timid smile. I quickly glanced back at the handsome man, but he was gone. I sighed and looked at this man with no name, who I felt I somehow knew. I refused to smile back. I didn't want to encourage conversation.

Poor guy, maybe he couldn't help but stare. I bet he made everyone else feel as uncomfortable as he did me. I didn't want to just dismiss him. I thought it would be unkind. Something kept me at that table, something more than just wanting to finish my omelette and latte. I was no psychic, or psychoanalyst, but by looking at his face I felt he may just have been riddled with even more pain and secrets than me. Of course, I wasn't going to pry, I wasn't going to find out about his life, because I didn't want to. Above all, I didn't want him to know about me. Yet I stayed there, and I surprised myself with how I looked right back at him as though I had no shame. Why should I move?

'Hello,' he said, and it seemed like he was attempting a smile again, but it still didn't look quite right.

'Hi,' I said, stone-faced.

He was silent for a while; his head drooped down and he was gazing at his hands, interlocked and resting on his lap. There was something about his voice that I didn't like, but I couldn't figure out what it was. He looked like he was either in his late sixties or even seventies; his skin was dark and leathery, perhaps the product of having lived on these sunny streets for so long. His hair was long, sparse, messy and grey. He was neither skinny nor particularly big. People-watching was fun but this had begun to feel too close for comfort. He looked up at me suddenly, with a sharp gaze that startled me.

'What's your name?' he said.

I was still stunned, and replied without thinking.

'Silvia,' I said.

'Silvia,' he repeated, and nodded slowly, as though deep in thought.

Oh god, I thought, *I know this game – you're now going to proceed to read my palm and tell me my future, right? Yaaawwwn.* But after that he was silent once again, not looking at me. Should I ask him his name? I was about to, but he looked up suddenly with his piercing, sad-kind eyes.

'Where are you from Silvia?'

This time I didn't feel so startled; after a little thought I decided that if I was going to tell anyone a bit about myself then this odd random stranger could certainly be that person. I smiled, almost laughed.

'Mexico,' I said, 'but my mother was Norwegian.'

Fuck. Why did I add the bit about my mother? I could have just said I'm half Norwegian, half Mexican, the usual spiel. Why did I have to go and mention her? Did it even matter? Why would it matter? He was just an old man who roamed the streets after all.

A strong gust of wind sent my napkin flying off the table, my body automatically followed to catch it. Suddenly the sky opened and rain started to pour down. I felt a sudden need to escape and the rain provided a perfect opportunity to do so. I looked back at him. He looked at me. I didn't say goodbye. As I ran home, attempting to shelter myself by weaving in and out under shop and restaurant awnings, I wondered about the rain and about the man and his tired, sad old eyes.

Meeting Jack

Thursday at noon I picked up my ringing phone and saw Pete's name come up.

'Hello?'

'Hi sweety, so sorry to do this last minute but I can't make it today after all.'

'Oh shit. Really?'

Damn, I'd really wanted to draw Pete today. I'd hyped myself up for it. But it was hardly a big deal, I'd just work from some previous sketches of him, or maybe do some more abstracts.

'Okay. No worries,' I continued.

'Yeah, but I do have someone who's keen to take my place, if you're interested?'

Oh, this was interesting. I wondered if this someone was plump, like him.

'He's a great guy. A friend of mine. He's a lawyer.'

'Okay. Yes. Actually that would be great.'

'His name's Jack. Really nice guy. I'll send you over his number in a sec.'

'Yeah, okay, thanks Pete. Any friend of yours is fine by me. You know where to send him.'

The doorbell rang at 2:04. Slightly late. Typical for a newcomer. I waited a few seconds and then went to answer it.

'Hello.'

'Hi.'

'Are you Silvia?'

'Yep, and you're Jack, right?'

For some reason I must have been expecting to open the door to a stocky, suit-clad middle-aged guy – a lawyer-type person – because I was more than a little surprised when I saw the man in front of me. He wasn't plump like Pete at all, he was tall and athletic looking. Maybe early thirties, thereabouts. His hair was dishevelled and dark, and he had an unshaven stubbly face, slightly crooked teeth, but a big wide smile. He was wearing a plain white loose t-shirt, dark tracksuit bottoms, trainers and a backpack. Perhaps he'd just come from the gym.

Usually, when I first met a guy, one of the first things I thought was whether I could imagine us having sex. Not because I was sex-obsessed but because friendships weren't an option in my life, so sex was the only pleasant thing a man could offer me. But today, I have to say, I didn't seem to care so much. Maybe it was because of that stupid pill. I'd opened up the leaflet that morning and had read the long list of potential side effects. Loss of sex drive was one of them. Depression and teariness were also thrown in there for good measure. Great.

'Come on in.'

'Thank you.'

'Thank you for stepping in for Pete by the way, especially at such short notice.'

'Oh no, that's totally fine. It's kind of a random thing for me to do, but I like random. I've actually often thought this is something I'd like to try in the future,' he paused and smiled at me, 'especially since Pete said he'd started doing it.'

I smiled back.

I liked him. It's not that I found him immediately attractive or anything like that. That's not what I mean. I liked his way of being. There was something relaxing about his presence, something I couldn't put my finger on, something that made me feel... good, that's all.

'Well,' I said, 'so long as you feel comfortable being naked, I don't think we have a problem.'

We both laughed.

'Well I can't say I'm not a little bit nervous, but yes, totally fine being naked.'

'Ah, there's a first time for everything,' I said, and then thought it sounded quite stupid. 'In any case you can turn the heater up and down as you please,' I continued, 'God, I remember the first time I ever did it I was freezing, so I vowed to myself that no one I ever drew would have to go through that!'

Oh god, was I rambling?

'Would you like a tea or coffee before we start?'

'No, I'm fine thank you,' he said, 'I have some water in my bag.'

'Ah okay, you just come from the gym?' I asked, continuing the pointless chit-chat.

'No, no, I'm not a gym person. I actually just came from an interview.' He glanced down at his clothes. 'I mean I dropped by home to get changed into something more comfortable. I hate suits. I have to wear them so often. It's silly really, no idea why they make us wear that stuff. Anyway... interview... yeah I've been working freelance for a while and now I'm looking for something more permanent. Yeah, so no, I wasn't at the gym.'

Now *he* was rambling.

'Oh yeah, you're a lawyer, aren't you? Pete mentioned.'

I immediately regretted saying it. I didn't particularly want to get into a conversation about what we did and who we were. He nodded and looked as though he was about to say something else, but I got there first: 'Okay. Well let me introduce you to the *stage*,' I said, faking a laugh.

I walked towards the large studio area: white sheets laid out across the floor and over the different levels of tables, stools, chairs and a mattress that made up the area where my subjects posed. Next to it stood a fan heater.

'This is a nice place,' he said.

That's what everyone said.

'Do you live here alone?'

'Yes,' I said, and then added, 'I won't be a minute!'

I rushed off to the bathroom to avoid any further questions. I didn't feel like being my usual blunt self with him, so this momentary escape from the situation felt like my best option.

That was always the way: *I don't need to know much about you, and you don't ask questions about me. Shallow stuff is okay, like what kind of tea I drink, or if I like it when they put jalapeños in salads, or if I think Leonardo DiCaprio is hot. That's fine. Trivial stuff is totally fine. If you're lucky I might even tell you I'm half Norwegian and half Mexican, but that's only if you dare ask, of course. What an interesting mix, you'll say. But other stuff, you know, stuff about my past, about my parents, how they met, if they live in this country, how on earth I afford such an expensive penthouse apartment... Don't bother.* Yet I knew they all wondered. I knew they all wanted to know how the hell a twenty-four-year-old girl could afford to live in such a place all by herself and still pay her clients a reasonable rate. I mean it's not like I was an overwhelmingly successful artist. Not that they had to know that, of course.

When I returned after a couple of minutes he seemed to not have taken my sudden departure as weird in the least bit.

'All right, so should I start getting, er, naked?' he said.

'Yes please!' I said as I reached over for some charcoal. 'And for the first sketch just do whatever you feel most comfortable with. Lie down, sit down, whatever, I honestly don't mind.'

He was new to this, and I liked him, so I definitely wanted to make sure he felt comfortable.

'I'll just let you know later on when and if I want you to change position,' I added.

'Okay, great, so I suppose you'll be forcing me to get into some kind of crazy yogic poses later then.'

'Oh yeah, obviously! I'm just easing you in.'

We laughed.

He stood there naked, looking down at the white sheets and hesitating for a second because he didn't know where to go. Then he chose the mattress and lay himself face down, propping his head up with his hands and staring out the window at the sky. That way, I got a view of the whole length of the left side of his lying body and a profile of his face. I could see how this would have been a comfortable option for him. There was no chance of his eyes meeting mine. At least he wasn't cocky – Max had been overly confident from the start, keen to have his penis staring at me confrontationally from the very first day.

He carried on staring at the sky for ages. It was interesting to watch him. He didn't say a word, but the silence wasn't awkward and it didn't seem to be coming from any kind of shyness or nervousness on his part. He didn't tell me anything about himself and didn't ask me any questions. It was interesting, and yet so strangely pleasant. I don't know why, but I just felt so happy and relaxed watching him. What an odd and surprising feeling it was. I had to watch myself though, what if he suddenly turned to look at me? I didn't want to be caught gazing and smiling at him. He'd think I was a pervert. But this had nothing to do with that. I just felt so untroubled and relaxed, like a child. How strange, yet how… lovely.

I looked at his face just as I was about to draw it and I realised that it had such a non-descript expression. He was just gazing at the sky in what seemed a very absent-minded way. There was no frown, no tension, no sign of worry. It was like he was sleeping with his eyes open. Could this be why I was feeling so good? Was there something in that relaxed face that was rubbing off on me? Who knew? But in any case I found myself smiling again.

After a few more poses and a few more sketches I asked him if he could put his clothes back on again.

'I just want to do some sketches in clothes as well,' I said.

I didn't always just draw naked people. The truth is I wanted to draw his face, because it fascinated me a little. It inspired me. Of course, I didn't tell him any of this because I was scared that if I did he'd suddenly become self-conscious and his expression would change.

People react differently to being naked in front of other people. Some people feel more comfortable with clothes on. I didn't know if he was that type. It was his first time after all. Though generally the people who decided to pose naked didn't seem to have a problem with it, and could be just as relaxed with or without their clothes. Some even seemed more relaxed in front of me when they were naked. I absolutely loved being naked. My human body was one of my greatest joys. I loved seeing it naked, feeling the smoothness and the curves. I loved it when my hair brushed my naked back. And I loved being naked with men, because I loved seeing the thing that I loved so much – my body – being enjoyed by others.

My body was the one thing I could share with others to bring them some kind of joy, which is why I loved and cherished it so much and why I had always shared it so freely. My mind was full of locked doors, but they couldn't stop me sharing my humanness in other ways. I still wanted to give some kind of joy to the world, and my body was one way I could do this. A direct portal to joy.

Jack put his clothes back on calmly, like he was the master of his own time; unfazed, in his own world. I watched him from the corner of my eye, whilst wiping charcoal off my hands. I asked him to sit himself on the chair and to get into a comfortable position.

The next hour was bliss. The rare moment came. The sun drifted in through the windows. Rays of light hit the room and the objects in it. Dust particles glistened like fairy dust. Everything was transformed and alive, and I became completely absorbed in the large white piece of paper that floated, totally alive, in front of my eyes. I made my markings on the page and breathed a new world – a new reality – onto it. I created. And yet, once again, just like in such previous moments, it felt as though it wasn't me who was drawing anymore. Drawing was simply happening. Those rare freeing moments of clarity and bliss that I experienced during the creative process were so powerful that, in an instant, they wiped away all the things I thought made me who I was. Flow.

I don't think I'd ever before succeeded in drawing such a satisfying portrait. The two hours were over. I made us tea. He wanted to see the drawings. I hesitated, but only out of habit, for I was more than happy to show this new model. I turned the easel towards him as he walked towards it. He stared at it and was silent for a while.

'Woah. That's incredible.'

He looked overwhelmed. Either he really was or he was good at faking it.

'Wow,' he said.

He was looking at me now and grinning.

'Thank you,' I said.

'That's amazing. Not to say I didn't expect it to be, but I just didn't know…'

I laughed. I didn't know whether to say it, as I thought he might think I was trying to make him feel special or something, but I said it anyway: 'Thanks, I think this may be one of my favourite pieces.'

'Can I see any of your other work?'

I hesitated, again out of habit. I mean, I suppose there was nothing to actually stop me from showing him. Why shouldn't I? I didn't have any secrets when it came to my art; I guess I just never showed many people, unless I was exhibiting of course.

'I used to draw when I was younger,' he said.

'Oh yeah? How come you stopped?'

He shrugged. 'Time, I guess.' He paused, and then he laughed. 'Whatever time is.'

I wasn't sure what he meant, but I didn't ask.

'I write sometimes though,' he said.

'Oh yeah? What kind of stuff?'

'Oh, well. I guess some people might call it poetry, but I don't know… there's usually no real structure to it. And I also dabble a bit with photography – especially underwater photography. But then, who isn't a photographer these days, right?' he said, and then, after a pause, he added, 'but in any case, it's nice to meet creative types.'

He looked at me and smiled. It seemed a warm thing to say, as though he was showing in some way that he liked me.

'So,' I said, 'how did you find your first life drawing session?'

'It's funny,' he said, 'sitting and lying around like that for such a long time with nothing to do gives you a lot of time to think about a lot of things that you don't usually get a chance to think about.'

'Oh really? That's strange, you looked like you weren't thinking about anything at all.'

'Really? Maybe because I was trying to meditate a bit as well,' he said, laughing – as though he was judging himself for it.

'Meditating?'

'Yeah. I'm using the term loosely though.'

'Did it work?'

'Hmm. Not really. Maybe a little. I don't know,' he paused, looking out the window. 'All I know is that I know nothing,' he mumbled. Then he looked at me again. 'Man, my mind's frazzled. Sorry, I forgot what I was saying.'

'Meditation.'

'Oh, yes. I have mixed feelings about it. But I don't quite know why I'm talking about that anyway,' he said, trying to brush it all off. 'This tea's lovely by the way, thank you.'

I was intrigued. I felt such a huge desire to talk to him. *Such* a huge desire. I had never felt something quite like this before. I didn't know whether it was to do with him, or me, or both of us. Fuck, it hurt so much. I wanted to cry. I would have given anything to be able to talk to him, and talk and talk and talk. Where had this sudden desire come from? I wanted to know his mind, more than I had ever wanted to know anyone else's. But I couldn't take without giving, could I?

We were silent for a while. And then something happened that I never in my life thought possible. Suddenly I felt I was stepping into a world that was both dangerous and exhilarating. And I didn't know how I felt about it, but I felt I was mad.

'Sounds like you have a lot on your mind?' I said.

It was just a question. A normal question. More of a statement than a question, in fact. But I knew what that question meant. It meant opening up. It meant: *you tell me about you, and I'll tell you about me.* It signified stepping into the unknown: a world that I didn't have planned out, a world I knew nothing about and that could end in far more hurt and fear for me. It could end in violence. But in a moment of madness I found myself stepping into this world again, after seventeen long years. And suddenly it felt as though I was falling, tumbling through a chasm, utterly terrified and yet so incredibly alive. This was total madness. I had lost my mind, and yet I felt life pulsating in every bit of my body and telling me that this was exactly what I needed to do. Adrenaline. And then I saw stars; I heard a smash as my cup fell to the ground, the room went black and I fainted. All because of one trivial little question.

Five minutes later I was lying on the sofa regaining consciousness.

'Thank god,' he said, letting go of my hand. 'I honestly thought I'd have to call an ambulance.' He smiled at me. 'You took your time.'

'Sorry,' I mumbled.

'Don't be silly. Are you okay?'

'Yeah.' I sat up suddenly. 'I'm so sorry, oh my god, how embarrassing.'

'No, no, don't say that, not at all, are you sure you're okay?'

'Yeah, yeah, I'm fine.'

This was the perfect opportunity to creep back to my usual silence, my world of secrets. It was the perfect distraction; we could easily forget I ever asked the question.

'Can I make you another tea?' he asked.

I glanced over to where my cup had fallen and smashed. He had cleared it all up.

'Thank you, that's really nice of you.'

Surely another cup of tea was fine, so long as I kept my mouth shut.

I watched him finding his way around the kitchen, answering when he asked where I kept the cups and the sugar. I wondered why he was still here. I mean perhaps it was obvious – after all I'd just fainted, maybe it would be rude of him to leave now. But still, the session had officially finished twenty minutes ago, and I'd already paid him. This was all very strange, and yet at the same time his presence felt so natural. He almost didn't feel like a stranger.

'Does that happen often?' he said, snapping me out of my thoughts.

'Sorry?'

'The fainting. Do you have low blood pressure or something?'

'No, I don't think so, I hardly ever faint.'

'I'll put lots of sugar in this tea in any case,' he laughed.

It suddenly occurred to me, 'You are making tea for yourself too, right? Please do. I mean only if you want to of course, but I don't imagine you actually got to finish the last one. Sorry about that.'

I tried to laugh and make it all sound very light-hearted.

'Sure. I could have another tea. Thank you.'

I waited in silence.

'That's an interesting scar you have on your hand,' he said, pouring milk into the cups – not looking over at me.

'Oh. Oh yes. An accident. I was taking down an exhibition and a glass frame shattered in my hands.'

'Ouch. Sounds painful.'

I didn't say anything.

He brought the cups over and put them on the coffee table. He sat down opposite me on the smaller sofa and took a sip. What was he doing here? He didn't know me and I didn't know him. Should this be strange? And yet it seemed to me as though he wanted to stay too, as though something was making him stay. Ah, I was being stupid, I was reading into things, making up a story in my head. After all, how could I possibly know what he was thinking? He was looking out of the window again. I looked out too. It was so clear, not a cloud.

'So what do you see when you stare out of that window?' I asked.

He laughed.

'Sorry,' he said, looking away from it, at me, and then at the cup in his hands.

'No don't be. I didn't mean that. I actually seriously want to know.'

'Ha! Really? What are you blind or something?' he joked.

'No. Colour-blind.'

'Really?'

'Yes.'

'Oh sorry,'

'Ha, don't be.'

'That's interesting. Partially? Totally?'

'Totally.'

I was doing this. I was actually doing this. I was telling someone. God it felt good... and terrifying. So terrifying.

'Black, white and shades of grey. That's my life,' I continued.

'From birth?'

My heart started pounding so fast it seemed it was about to explode. I shook my head.

'No.'

Silence.

'Oh god,' I said, registering the intrigue on his face, 'I actually don't feel too good after all.' To add to my act I started fanning myself with a random bit of junk mail lying on the coffee table. 'I'm sorry, I don't know what's wrong with me today. I think it's probably best I get some sleep.'

'Of course,' he nodded, trying his best to replace his intrigue with concern. 'If there's anything I can do to help...'

'No, no. But thank you.'

'Well you should at least let a friend or family member know, have them check in on you, okay?'

Ha! Friends and family. What a joke. But I nodded. And I tried to smile to reassure him that I was okay, even though I wasn't.

'Thanks so much for filling in for Pete at such short notice, I'm so happy with how the drawings came out.'

He smiled, nodded, but didn't say anything. I made to get up but he stopped me and, after a short awkward exchange of goodbyes, he let himself out. And I was left lying on that sofa, watching steam rise from the two cups of tea on the coffee table, and wondering what the fuck had just happened.

That evening I realised I could no longer keep the secrets.

An Imagined Life

I liked Balboa Park. It was the perfect mix. I could spend hours in the manicured gardens with their fresh green scent, and all those carefully placed trees, plants and flowers made me feel normal. A normal member of society. And, with all its art galleries and museums, Balboa Park was, above all, a place I came to for inspiration. Balboa had its wilder parts too. And I loved those parts the most. It was in those parts that I'd had some of my most interesting walks, often in states of deep reflection.

Today would be a Balboa day. Really, you could spend a whole day there. I'd start off south by Inspiration Point lot – not the best entry point for where I was headed, but how fitting a name. I always started there. Call it superstition.

I wouldn't bother with the park's tram; today was a day for walking and thinking, and I wasn't in a rush. I'd follow the usual plan, starting at the Museum of the Living Artist, followed by the Museum of Man and the Museum of Art, then moving to the Timken Museum of Art, then the Museum of Photographic Arts and the Natural History Museum. Then I'd wind my way that little bit extra north for a stop off at the Spanish Village Art Centre. There was so much – almost too much – to see in this stretch of San Diego land. Once I had those done, if I wasn't too exhausted, I had space for spontaneity. Sometimes this meant a visit to a random museum, but more often than not it meant having lunch or coffee in one of the cafés, and a rest in one of the botanical gardens to breathe in an intoxicating tangle of aromas. But I would always end my Balboa day with a walk.

Staring at Monet's 'Haystacks at Chailly at Sunrise' , I found myself deep in thought. I thought about Norway – how much I still craved going there one day, even though that same thought made me feel sick to my stomach. I vividly remembered a photo my mother had showed me when I was little of a field of haystacks. I couldn't remember which part of Norway it was and why she had that photo but I could remember them looking just like the haystacks in this painting. The lighting would have been pretty similar too. I remembered warm golden hues as the early morning sun reflected off every blade of hay. Of course, at that moment, those colours were only something I could imagine in Monet's painting. What had he been thinking all those years back when he stood in front of his haystack muse? Awe at the warm burst of colour the rising sun was bringing to the landscape? Hope at the dawn of a new day? Of the stillness in the early hours of the morning? Or was he preoccupied with something totally unrelated? I had read once that he'd had some difficulty persuading the conservative Académie des Beaux-Arts to exhibit his work in the Salon de Paris, so maybe as he stared at those haystacks he was just pissed off about that. His mind could have been anywhere, I knew that. In fact, right then, was a perfect example. I had been standing there in front of that painting for at least fifteen minutes, absorbed in my thoughts, when I suddenly felt a presence next to me, and…

'Silvia!'

Shit, what was his name?

'Oh my god, Jack, hello!'

Of course I knew his name – my split-second memory lapse was just the result of snapping out of a daydream. Jack had certainly been on my mind.

'What are you doing here?' I asked.

He let out an embarrassed laugh. 'I've just come from a date.'

I glanced at my watch. An early date; that had ended early by the looks of it too. It couldn't have gone that well. Unless he'd spent last night with her.

'Oh. That's nice.'

'And you? What are you doing here?'

'Oh me, I come here often. Inspiration station and all that.'

'Of course,' he nodded and looked up at Monet's piece. 'And do you always stare at this one painting for so long?'

Had he been watching me?

'Er, no. I just got lost in thought.'

'Well it's good to see you're better. I was actually waiting to hear back from Pete about you. I wanted to get your number to check up on you.'

'Oh that's real nice. I'm totally fine now, thank you.' A small smile melted my nerves.

'I was just about to go grab a coffee, if you'd like to join me?'

Coffee meant conversation, and conversation was dangerous. But I spoke before reflecting on this.

'Sure, why not.'

It was okay, I'd just make sure that he was the one talking. And, if he asked about me, I'd stick to talking about art. *It's fine*, said the voice in my head, but my quickened heartbeat seemed to indicate otherwise.

I hated small talk, but it was the only thing I had access to, and this silence while we walked to the café was making my palms sweat.

'So, how was the date?'

There was his embarrassed laugh again.

'Ah, it was okay, thank you. But I think we kind of clash.'

'Oh, how come?'

'Well, it might seem silly, but, for example, she works in fashion, and at heart, I'm just too much of a raging anti-consumerist for that.'

I laughed and nodded. I was smiling. It was torture to find myself once again enjoying his company.

It was a cloudless day, so we decided on a take-out coffee and a walk. Never had I been accompanied on any of my visits here. In fact, it had been ages since I'd been accompanied by anyone in public at all. This was big. I was both scared and exhilarated. I felt like a rebel, but a terrified one. I found myself looking over my shoulder every few minutes. What if they were watching me? *No Silvia, get that thought out of your head, there's nothing bad happening here. This is all innocent. Jack will do the talking, you don't have to say anything. You're in control. You set the rules.*

'So,' he said as we walked beneath the shade of Balboa Park's huge fig tree, 'you're colour-blind.'

I choked on my coffee.

'Sorry,' he said, noticing his lack of subtlety.

For a moment I didn't say anything; I didn't nod, I didn't shake my head. I just looked straight ahead and tried to swallow my coffee in a dignified way. This walk had been a really bad idea. And now I needed to think how I would steer the focus back on to him.

'Sorry,' he said again, 'I was just thinking about where we left off the other day—'

'But wait, we were going to talk about you first.'

'We were?'

'Yes. Before I so rudely fainted that day I think you were going to tell me what was on your mind.'

'I was?'

How would I control this conversation? We were in the middle of a walk, and there was no way out except running away. And running away was not an option. And, deep down, I actually wanted to stay.

'Yeah, I'm pretty sure you had something on your mind that day.'

'I did. But I really wouldn't want to bore you with it.'

There was silence again. I looked at him. My guess was that he was about to tell me about some kind of devastating break-up, and I would have to feign pity. But that would be perfect; we could focus entirely on him and his despair.

'I get the feeling we both have somewhat strange minds at the moment,' he said.

'Oh?'

'Well,' he shrugged, 'life – it's a funny thing. That's all.'

What did he mean by that? And how had he assumed that I had a strange mind? Was I that obvious?

'I don't know why I'm even tempted to start telling you all this,' he continued. 'In a sense there's really nothing to talk about. I guess this is just that typical thing of feeling comfortable in a stranger's presence.'

Oh, so that was a typical thing?

'Not that you're a total stranger anymore, but you know what I mean... someone I don't really know all that well. Yes, but, anyway, I don't really know how to formulate my thoughts into words. It's all a long story, in a sense. God, this is like a shrink session or something,' he laughed.

'Just tell me. Tell me everything.' I said without thinking, because I was far too scared of where more silence might take us.

'Okay. I will.'

He laughed, probably at the absurdity of it all – wondering to himself why on earth he was about to open up to a stranger. I laughed too, but because my body was crippled with nerves. And the eyes that looked on him as he began to speak were eyes of longing. I longed to be an equal participant in our strange encounter. I too longed to tell him everything.

'What I'm about to tell you is incomprehensible, so don't worry if you don't understand. I don't either.' He paused and looked to the side. 'See?' he said, 'It already sounds weird. I'm really bad at talking about it, words seem to ruin it somehow, but bear with me, I'll try to say it as succinctly as I possibly can. But I can assure you it won't be succinct.'

I was no longer sure that he was about to pour his heart out over a recent break-up. Maybe this was actually about something else. Either that, or the break-up had affected him pretty bad. But let's just say I suddenly felt intrigued. And calmer, now that the attention was all on him.

'I'm originally from the east coast. Long Island. That's where I grew up. I moved to San Diego to study, ten years ago. I had to take a two-year break first, and work like a dog in New York, to afford to move here and study. I met one of my closest friends, Adam, at college. We were on the same course. We were involved in a lot of different movements in our college years and up until our mid twenties. We met some people, did some stuff… I don't need to go into the details, but it was all pretty radical. The government didn't like people like us.' he shrugged.

The government? I wanted to stop him, but I didn't.

'Anyway,' he continued, 'that was all a while ago and it didn't last that long. It seemed to peak at the end of one summer… five years ago. Along with some other stuff. Again, I don't need to go into the details of what was going on in my life round that time but it suffices to say I was worrying a lot about a few different things. So,' he paused, 'and this is the part I find hard to talk about, not because it's too personal or anything like that, but because truly words fail me…'

'Yes,' I said, 'go on.'

'Well, I was back in New York that fall, visiting my parents and my sister. I was walking along an empty beach in Montauk one day, by myself. I think I'd just been in for a swim, and wanted to take a long walk to dry off.' He glanced at my reaction and quickly added, 'I love wild swimming, and I've been pretty obsessed with cold water swimming since I was a kid.'

I smiled and nodded but remained silent so as not to distract him further.

'Anyway,' he continued, 'that day my mind was on a lot of different things, I'd had a fight with my dad that morning, and I was probably thinking about all sorts of stuff while walking along that beach. But then, suddenly, everything changed.'

'What changed?'

'Everything. It was as though everything dropped away and I looked up and all I saw was the miracle. I suddenly realised that life, that everything was an utter mind-blowing miracle.'

I found myself laughing, then realised he was being totally serious.

'It was extraordinary,' he said. 'It's like my understanding of the word *life* suddenly got turned on its head. Suddenly it occurred to me that absolutely nothing mattered. All was well. So well. See, I know that sounds stupid. Probably sounds like a load of hippy shit to you.'

I shook my head and urged him to continue.

'But the thing is I had never ever before in my life thought about any spiritual stuff. I mean—'

'So wait, you're saying this was a spiritual experience?'

'Well I hate that word, but I don't really know what else to call it. What I mean is like I didn't even know the meaning of words like *enlightenment* or *awakening* or anything like that. I'd just never in my life been interested in that stuff, you know? Only later, when I read some books that kind of helped me understand the experience, did I learn those words.' He sighed. 'I guess I'm just trying to say that I didn't have some kind of spiritual hippy background before this happened. So it was all the more random, and maybe because of that all the more powerful.'

'And you weren't on anything?'

He knew straight away what I meant. He laughed. Well, it was only fair of me to ask – I had to rule out the options.

'No,' he said.

'So was it like a *satori*? Like an awakening?'

He raised his eyebrows, 'Yes, I think that might be the right word, how do you know about that stuff?' He sounded surprised.

'It's hard not to when you live in California.'

By that I really only meant that I'd once stumbled across an article about meditation and t'ai chi in a free women's health magazine, and I definitely remembered the words *enlightenment, satori* and *awakening* being mentioned. I secretly applauded my smug little self for impressing him with my vocabulary. But, the thing was, I actually then remembered that it had been an interesting article; perhaps it had reminded me of what it was like to be a very young child.

'Though I can't say I've ever had such a big defining awakening moment myself,' I added. 'I mean, probably except when I was really little or something. You know, because kids tend to—'

'Live in that state non-stop?'

'Yeah. Completely.' I smiled at his ability to end my sentence.

He was clearly quite happy – and perhaps even a little impressed – that I understood some of what he was saying, so I decided to go further.

'And, I mean, I don't know if this is entirely related, but sometimes when I'm drawing or painting I get into a state of flow. It's an incredible feeling, everything just drops away and there's just me and the paper, and everything else that I usually think is so real, y'know, like my life, my story and all that, just ceases to exist. I forget it all. It stops being real and important because the only thing that's real is what's happening. And it feels very… blissful, I guess,' I shrugged, 'and relaxed, so relaxed.'

He was nodding.

'But yeah, sorry, continue,' I said.

'Well, I guess mainly that's all that happened – just this sudden epiphany. But there were also other realisations that came with it. I suddenly wondered why the hell I had ever worried about anything before, why and how I could have ever allowed myself to suffer over anything. It seemed absurd to me that I could ever go through any mental trauma when *this*, this miracle, was so obviously staring me in the face and life was the most incredible thing ever, and there was nothing to worry about.'

He suddenly stopped and looked at me.

'I do realise that maybe all this could somehow sound airy-fairy or something,' he said, 'but I'll say it anyway, because I may as well give you as best a description of what happened as I can… I looked at the sky, the clouds, the rays of light, the sand, grass, trees, birds, the sea – that strange mass of a thing called water – and I had a clear, deep feeling that I was not separate from any of it. Though I don't really know how to explain or describe that now, at the time it was so utterly clear. It was beyond understanding. There was a knowledge there that was totally beyond the logical mind. It was unquestionable. I guess deep down, on an atomic level, everything is the same, and maybe I just directly experienced the oneness of it all. I actually felt it. I looked around me and I felt such a deep sense of gratitude for simply being alive, for experiencing this miracle called life. And here's where the real hippy shit comes out,' he laughed, 'I felt something that I can only think to call love, an unconditional and limitless love.' He paused. 'You know, you hear all this stuff about how you have to suffer for love… but fear is the opposite of love. In my experience love is joy and freedom.'

Jack raised one eyebrow and looked at me as though he was once again about to self-deprecate for sounding kind of new-agey. But I was nodding so enthusiastically, that instead he continued.

'And sometimes you think you're in love but actually you're just in love with an idea, an idea of someone, an idea of how they are or how you want them to be. But it's just an idea. It's not who they are…'

Yes. That made sense. Perhaps my mother had been in love with an idea she held of my father, Diego, an idea she'd been desperately clinging onto since she first met him. I wanted Jack to elaborate on his theory of love, but he continued in his own way.

'And also, I felt freedom, utter boundless freedom. I remember thinking that even if I was in a prison cell the freedom would be the same. So it wasn't freedom in the usual sense, not the sort of freedom that's determined by external conditions and circumstances, but an inner freedom, without conditions. Unconditional. And I felt joy. Total unadulterated child-like joy and wonder. I'd never felt anything like that in my life.' He had a big smile on his face. He looked as though he was reminiscing the feeling as he talked of it. 'And that's it, you see, I guess that's the point, because for a moment my so-called life stopped, and there was *just* life. Not *my* life, 'Jack's life', but just *life*. You said before that sometimes when you draw suddenly the only thing that seems real is what's happening. That's it. In that moment I saw that only life was happening, and I saw it to be a miracle.'

He stopped. He looked so enthusiastic that I couldn't help but grin back at him. There was something contagious about his full-faced smile. For a moment I forgot all about my own story and I actually felt a glimmer of happiness.

'This probably all sounds like a jumble of words that don't make any sense,' he said.

I shook my head.

'You know,' he said, 'it's funny because… well, it's hard to talk about. I mean, it's hard to put into words. I end up using words like spiritual, divine, mystical and all those types of words, to try describe it, but I don't want to use those words.'

'Why?'

'Because of what they connote. Those words can easily conjure up images of stuff that this has nothing to do with. Like, I mean, what happened was concrete. It wasn't anything like floating around in a different world, seeing angels and saints, feeling dreamy or anything like that. It was the opposite. It was so obvious and clear. It was like I finally *wasn't* dreaming. It was like suddenly waking up from a dream. It wasn't oblivion or a momentary switching off. It was total awareness and presence and suddenly switching on. Completely. For once in my life I was actually fully present in it. I couldn't believe I'd been asleep for so long. So the words, they just seem… I don't know, they make it seem religious or abstract. I don't know, maybe I'm wrong to think like that, but I guess I just don't feel totally comfortable using them.'

'So you feel that words kind of limit you?'

'Yes, I've often thought that.'

'But you write, don't you?'

He laughed. 'Maybe that's my way of trying to fight it, experimenting with words. Maybe the more I experiment the better I'll be able to express all this. I don't know.'

'I wouldn't worry too much about words. You can't please everyone.'

'That's true. I'm probably just overthinking it all.' He paused. 'Anyway, I guess I've just been listing some of the stuff I remember realising and feeling at the time. There's too much to say, and yet the more I say, the more I feel like I'm getting further away from describing the essence of what happened.'

'It doesn't matter,' I said, 'just say it.'

'Okay, I will.' He took a deep breath and continued. 'One of the other significant things that I came to realise is something I probably find hardest to talk about, firstly because I always get judged for saying it. If and when I do tell anyone this, no one can even begin to comprehend it. And secondly because, whilst it was so clear and obvious to me at the time, now that I'm back in the world of my mind and my life, even I find it hard to come to terms with…'

'Well… go on. What was it?'

'Basically, I realised that all the world's suffering, all the destruction, it was all just… a dream.'

What the fuck is he talking about? 'Sorry, what?'

'Yes, I know. See what I mean? Incomprehensible. It's not like a belief system of mine, or something I came to believe after thinking about stuff, or some kind of conclusion I came to after reading about stuff, actually it's quite the reverse, because everything I've ever been about, and still pretty much am about, everything I've ever believed in, everything I stand for is the complete opposite of that, you know? So it's not something I *believe*, it's just something that I briefly but somehow deeply realised while I was walking down that beach. Everything's a dream. We're living in a dream. Whether I get it or not right now, it was obvious and clear at the time. Whatever it means. And that's the hardest part to explain, because I can't even articulate it properly to myself.'

He paused.

'That's a very dangerous thing to go broadcasting around,' I said.

'Well of course. And it's not the sort of thing you *would* go broadcasting around to everyone. Because that's the thing – in the world as we know it, in life as we know it, it makes no sense at all. In fact, it's almost an *un*truth. You see, when I say it's all just a dream, I don't mean it in the way of *let's go torture and kill someone because who cares, it doesn't matter anyway, their suffering is an illusion and clearly not real, so it doesn't matter*. That's not what I mean. Within the dream suffering is real. Very real. And I suppose that's why I'm still so driven to try stop it.' He stopped for a second again. 'I can't explain it. I just can't. I don't think I'll ever be able to put it into words. Forget I said it. I already regret saying it.'

I wish he could have explained it. What was this dream he was talking about?

'But anyway,' he continued, 'you can see how that could have later made it hard to go back to the world of *my life*. Especially as a human rights and environmental lawyer.'

I nodded. And then I registered. A human rights and environmental lawyer? What the hell? It was as though life was playing games with me and shoving an answer to all my problems right in front of me. But no, it couldn't be that simple. No fucking way. I wasn't going to tell him anything. A secret is a secret. I blew that thought out of my mind and carried on listening to him as intensely as I could. It was a good distraction.

'You know what?' he said. 'War, torture, environmental destruction, murder, rape, hate crimes, greed, self hate, all of it, all the million problems of society – they're all just symptoms of this madness.'

'What madness?'

'Well…' he laughed, 'it's madness, isn't it? All these things we do. No other species on the planet is as destructive and dangerous as we are.'

God, he was starting to sound like my mother.

'I'm not saying it's good or bad,' he said, 'it's just plain insanity. Trapped in our deluded minds and identities, we're blinded. We can't see the fundamental magic of existence, and so we try to find some kind of magic we can claim as our own *within* it. We struggle for it, we suffer for it, we fight for it, we kill for it. We go through life looking for a treasure within it, without realising that life *itself* is the treasure. And at the same time we say we hate the wars, the destruction, all of that, and we go crazy trying to change the world by addressing each and every symptom…'

'So, what, are you saying we shouldn't try to change the world? We should just sit back, relax, and let all that shit happen?'

'No. I'm just pointing out that until we address the root of it all, none of it *will* change, not in the long run,' he paused, and then laughed, 'though I do think that if we were capable of sitting back and relaxing a bit more the world would be a better place.'

'Sounds to me like you're a Buddhist.'

He laughed. 'No. Not all. I'm definitely not a Buddhist. I don't have any philosophical beliefs or ideologies.'

I didn't say anything. For a few moments we just carried on walking and drinking our coffees in silence.

'You know, you don't need beliefs to realise that the mere fact there is something called *existence* in the first place is ridiculous,' he said, interrupting the silence. 'It's mind-blowing. It's crazy. And yet we don't see that.'

'Well, no, I disagree; I think sometimes we do. People wonder about why we're here and what the world is and how the universe came to be. I mean that's where science and religion come from in the first place.'

'Sure. Some of us get moments of pondering and wondering. But fundamentally, on a daily basis, we don't see or feel it. You know, the thing about the miracle of existence is that if and when people stop to ponder it they think of it as something happening in the past, either the Big Bang or God creating the world, or whatever, depending on their belief systems. And they're like, "Yeah, it's amazing that it happened, but so what? What's it got to do with me? It happened ages ago, and currently I have more pressing things to think about." But it's not got anything to do with what happened back then, *if* it happened, *why* it happened or *how* it happened. It's *this*, what's happening *now*. It's what's sustaining it. This is the miracle. That this is happening right now is not the product of a miracle that happened at the beginning of time. It *is* the miracle happening right now. It's crazy. It's beautiful. And when you suddenly see it, it's like *woah*, how could I not have? There are no words.'

'And you're sure you're not on something?'

We both laughed.

'No. Totally sure. I mean unless there's something in this coffee.'

'Well, would you mind swapping with me? I want some of whatever it is you have in there.'

I couldn't believe I was engaging like this with someone. God, it felt good.

'But you know, the thing is,' he continued, 'I also realised that all my angst, all my turmoil and anger, all my suffering over the suffering of others and the destruction of the planet, was redundant. It was never going to solve a thing. In fact, by feeling that way, I was actually just throwing out more suffering into the world. It was just another symptom of the madness. So, in a way, what happened actually helped me with my work, because I had a clearer head. I felt as though I could do all the things I'd used to do but without all the rage and negativity inside me. I seemed to get more done.'

'And all your anger and frustration, it just suddenly dropped away? With no conscious effort on your part?'

'Yes. Pretty much. But it did really shake stuff up for me. It made me rethink a lot of things. At first it kind of seemed to bring tension into my friendship with Adam. We'd been through a lot of stuff together and we'd understood each other so well on that level. But the thing about him is he had a bit of a past that I only much later found out about, of dabbling in all sorts of stuff, including eastern philosophy, psychedelic drugs, meditation, stuff like that.'

'All that hippy shit stuff, right?' I said, smirking. He laughed. 'Hey, I'm just using your words,' I said.

'Sure you are. And obviously you're totally judging me on all this.'

'Sure I am, you fucking hippy. So anyway, what happened to Adam?'

'Well, luckily his adventures have made it easier for him to finally understand some of the stuff I talk about. At the beginning though, he used to try to get into a lot of arguments with me about it. It was kind of tough because at the time he was really one of the only people I felt I could share all this with. But after a while, and in his own way, he seemed to come to terms with a lot of the stuff I'd told him. With a combination of yoga, surfing and living the simple California life, he mellowed out.'

He smiled, and I smiled back.

'Anyway, what happened on that beach that time was powerful. It was life changing. It's been with me ever since, except now it's just a memory, a very powerful one of course, I mean sometimes I get glimpses, but I'm very much a human being trapped in this world called my life story again, you know, albeit with a hell of a lot more perspective.'

'Yeah,' I said, and before I could stop myself, 'I know something about feeling trapped in a life story.'

God Silvia, no.

I could sense him looking right at me, perhaps even raising an eyebrow. He was clearly about to say something, but I managed to get there first.

'Oh my gosh,' I cast a quick blind glance at my watch, 'I'm so sorry, I didn't realise that was the time!' I racked my brain for the next part of the lie, 'I have to be back home in half an hour.' Bullshit, there was no way I'd make it back in half an hour. He knew that. 'I… I have someone coming round… for a session… in an hour.'

This lie, it was appalling, but it saved me.

I felt guilty. He'd just opened up to me. We weren't finished, we just weren't finished, damn it! But if I stayed any longer…

God! What was happening? Why had I even gone this far with Jack, and why did I want to continue? Here I was, dismissing it all so suddenly with a goddamned shit lie. It felt terrible.

'I'm sorry for taking up your time,' he said. It sounded more like a question than a statement.

'No no. I'm sorry. How stupid of me,' I didn't dare look him in the eyes. I was far too embarrassed. 'I feel awful. I'm really sorry. I was really enjoying your company,' I blurted out and then felt even more embarrassed.

'Likewise. I don't usually talk about the stuff I just talked about with you… so sorry if I went off on one,' he said.

Shit, now I felt really guilty.

'Fuck, no Jack. It was all so fascinating.' I meant it, I really meant it. God only knew I wished we could have carried on.

We stood there for a few more seconds in idiotic silence. I looked around trying to get my bearings. Which way was best to run?

'Well I think I'll just carry on walking,' he said, 'I won't keep you any longer for now.'

For now?

'Thanks Jack. Enjoy your walk. Goodbye.'

I turned round, and, without looking back, I ran.

That Smile

The thing about the mind is that it has a life of its own. And mine had developed a habit of thinking about Jack. I knew I had already gone too far with him, but even so – or perhaps because of it – I found myself fantasising about hypothetical conversations with him.

I was on my way to meet Polly, my dealer, and more than anything I wished I could have just sat down with her and asked for her opinion. You know, like they do in the movies. People have heart-to-hearts in the movies. People share secrets, open up. I wanted to tell her about Jack.

'How's school, Polly?' I asked, after we'd greeted each other in the abandoned parking lot – our usual meeting place. She smelled different today, like perfume. The smell was subtle, but it was totally unlike her, so it hit me.

'Ah, y'know, okay, I guess.'

'Almost the end now, isn't it?'

'Mmm yeah.'

She was smiling. A kind of shy but super excited grin. It looked like she was using every muscle of her face to try and hold it in. Even I knew what that grin meant. 'Have you met a boy Polly?' I smiled at her.

She half frowned, but then immediately forgave my mistake and was beaming again.

'A girl, actually,' she said.

'Oh sorry. My bad.'

'Yeah, she's rad. Really rad. I mean, it's like only the beginning and stuff…'

Yes, it's always exciting at the beginning, isn't it? I thought. 'Ah, but still… that's exciting!' I said.

'Mmm, yeah,' she nodded, trying so hard to contain that smile.

She handed me the carefully-prepared bag of weed, with my name handwritten on it in her pretty handwriting. I handed her the cash. She was still nodding. She was always quite highly sprung, but this time I could tell it was induced more by circumstance than by chemicals.

'We're thinking of going away together for the summer,' she said.

'Oh, nice! What's her name?' I wondered where I would score my weed if Polly disappeared all summer.

'Olivia.'

As she said this, Polly looked deep into my eyes with a piercing excited gaze that told me she was desperate to carry on talking about Olivia.

Who was I to give relationship advice? Unlike most other people I dealt with, though, Polly was one person I didn't feel too nervous about engaging in a bit of conversation. I didn't see her too often so I felt it was totally okay to lie to her if I had to. But who'd have thought we'd wind up sitting in a concealed corner of the lot, our backs perched against a wall and our butts pressing into the gravelly ground, sharing a joint?

After what seemed like an hour discussing Olivia, Polly's previous relationships, what it meant to be a good girlfriend and, above all, sex, I had somehow managed to steer the conversation onto Jack. I don't know how. I shrugged off The Fear. *Fuck it Silvia, it's only Polly,*

I told myself. I felt so relaxed. I didn't reveal much about myself of course; I was still sober enough to not make that mistake. But I found myself coming towards the end of a delirious – yet hushed, always hushed – babble about Jack's epiphany and the strange sense of calm he'd made me feel the first day I'd met him. I didn't tell her, of course, that I had no intention of seeing him again.

'So, what's holding you back?' Polly said.

'What d'you mean?'

'Well, have you fucked him yet?'

'God no. I mean, no Polly, I don't want to do that.'

Polly laughed. She laughed real hard.

'What?'

'Bullshit. Why the fuck are you talking about him then, if he's not someone you wanna screw?'

'No. Well that's the thing. It's not like that. I can't stop thinking about him but it's really not like that. If it was I would have fucked him already.'

We burst out laughing, but I felt bad for doing it. I didn't like the idea of 'fucking' Jack. He wasn't someone you just 'fucked'. I had too much… of something for him. I don't know what. Admiration, respect, perhaps.

'Look Silvia, you're hot. You should just fuck him.'

I was high, so high, as I walked home. I was flattered that dear seventeen-year-old Polly thought I was hot. My highness meant the absence of all my sadness and I loved it. Oh god bless you weed! I could have kissed the world right then!

I pulled my phone out of my pocket and scrolled to Jack's number.

But I didn't call him. Not that time.

The Perfect Excuse

It was another one of those freak days today: Arthur in the afternoon, Max in the evening. I'd seen Arthur earlier that week already – he'd received some negative feedback from one of his art tutors and had been in a foul mood, so to be frank, I was really not looking forward to seeing him again.

I had become very immersed in my art lately, and had managed to wean myself off constant thoughts about Jack. And, although I wasn't much looking forward to Arthur, I found myself looking forward to Max. I felt the need for some mindless sex today. All the things I'd started to hate about Max – today I craved them again. And, no doubt, I would have them.

At around noon, as I was cutting carrots into chunks to make a soup, my phone rang. Arthur.

'Morning Silvia.'

'Morning,' I said, even though it wasn't, anymore. 'What's up?'

He cleared his throat, 'Sorry Silvia, I don't feel too good today, I don't think I can make it.'

Arthur had never cancelled before. By the sounds of it he was hungover, but I didn't bother to pry, it wasn't in my nature.

'Sorry for the short notice.'

'It's okay.' It *was* okay. After all, I didn't really want to see him anyway. 'Hope you get better.'

'Thanks Silvia.'

'Okay. Bye.'

'Bye.'

The moment I hung up, my mind catapulted straight back to Jack. This was the perfect excuse I had been waiting for. He probably wouldn't be free at such short notice, but that wasn't the point – the point was to make contact.

Jack: the mysterious character that, against all my will, I was being drawn towards. He had imparted to me an inexplicable sense of possibility. But possibility of what, I didn't know. Such feelings were dangerous. It was easy to get too comfortable, lose self-control and say too much. And yet, even as I mulled this over, my fingers were typing a text message to him. I pressed send and felt a pang of fear, followed by a sense of relief. I didn't know which of those two feelings to trust, so instead I carried on chopping carrots.

As I switched off the blender I realised my phone was ringing. I honestly hadn't expected him to get back to me so soon. I let it ring for a few seconds longer and then I picked up.

'Hey,' I said.

'Hey. How are you? I just got your message.'

'Oh yeah, sorry about the short notice. I just thought y'know, if you're around and free and feeling up for it, then that'd be great, but I realise it's a pretty big ask, so...'

'Well, actually, I just had an interview a few blocks down from you, so I'm in the area. I was just about to head home, but... I don't know. I mean you need someone for 2pm, is that right?'

I looked at the clock. It was 12:30 exactly.

'Well... I mean not really. I was just about to have lunch. Have you eaten? I've made carrot and coriander soup.'

I honestly felt that there were two Silvias operating in me: the one who was doing all this talking, all this action, and the one who was observing her in fear, trying to scream to her *no, don't!*

'No, I haven't eaten yet. But are you sure?'

'Yes.'

Breaking Bread

He looked so different in a suit. Quite handsome. I didn't usually find suits all that appealing.

So, here we were at the dining table, filling the first few moments of silence with the crunch of breaking baguette and the slurping of hot soup. He looked away to the side and out of the windows.

'This really is such a great place you have here.'

'Thanks,' I said, and immediately changed the subject. 'You know, I've been thinking a lot about our conversation in Balboa Park the other week.'

'You mean my monologue?' he laughed.

'Yep. It was a good monologue.'

'Oh really? I'm glad you think so. Anything in particular?'

'Well, all of it, really. I've become very focused on my art since then. Maybe more than I have been in a while. I've been creating quite a lot of abstract pieces. When I do abstract stuff it means I'm not working with any concept, plan or formula in mind. It means I work in free flow. I guess really it's my favourite way of working, it's just I don't usually give myself much time for it, because the abstracts don't seem to sell all that well. Anyway. The point is that it's when I do the abstracts that I most often get those moments of flow I mentioned to you. And this week has been full of that.'

I could feel my face beaming. Even just recalling those moments of flow made me happy. He was beaming right back, with a look in his eyes that told me he knew exactly what I was talking about. I felt that crazy sense of possibility take over me again, like anything was possible.

I didn't mention that the copious amounts of weed I'd consumed that week had definitely added to those moments of flow, of letting go, losing myself. Perhaps I could have, but what with that suit he was wearing and the official and lawyer-esque air he had about him today, I decided not to.

'Obviously there's parts of your experience I don't understand,' I said.

'Of course. It's not something that can be understood.' He shook his head. 'It's beyond the intellect. Like I said, *I* don't even understand it.'

'Yeah. I see what you mean. But then, even if it can't be understood, there are parts of it that… well, they resonate… y'know?'

I fell in love with the smile that appeared on his face at that moment. I would have liked to capture it and keep it in my pocket as a go-to image for the rest of my life. All I could do was take a snapshot with my mind's eye.

Any moments of silence that followed whilst we finished lunch no longer felt so awkward. It was like an ice had been broken, and an unspoken bond had been established. It was wonderful, but there was a limit to all this, and soon our bonding would reach a plateau, because at some point the spotlight would have to turn on me and I couldn't let that happen, could I?

*

Oh god, he was doing it again. That relaxed face. Those eyes, distant yet present. As his naked body reclined on the white sheets he seemed to be once again surrounded by an invisible aura of calm. And, just as before, it was contagious.

'Silvia…'

'Mmm?'

'Do you ever paint in colour?'

Fuck. Why did I ever tell him about my colour-blindness? He wasn't going to let it go.

'No.'

He kept quiet after that and let me continue my work in silence.

An hour and a half later I felt I was done. Satisfied. After clothing himself he walked over to my easel, uninvited but not unwelcome, while I added the last touch to the drawing.

'Left-handed,' he said. 'Should have known. All the good ones are.' He looked at the drawing again and nodded. 'I like it.'

'Thanks,' I said. 'Tea?'

I really shouldn't have offered any; I really should have let him go.

'That'd be lovely, thank you.' He went back to look at the drawing again. 'Don't you ever wonder what it would be like if you did work in colour?'

'Don't be silly. It'd be shit. I'd never know what the final piece looked like.'

'But maybe that could be kind of fun. Kind of liberating. I think it'd be interesting.'

He was beating round the bush. I knew he wanted to know when and how and why I became colour blind. *This tea might be a big mistake,* I thought. And yet, some part of me felt it wasn't.

I suddenly felt under an immense amount of pressure. It was as though this moment was the deciding moment. Once the tea was ready, I placed the teacups on two saucers, put them on the coffee table and excused myself to go to the bathroom. I needed the time to think without him there looking at me. I sat down on the toilet seat. I cried. Was I really about to do this?

I felt safe with him. But maybe I was fooling myself. Maybe this was a trick of my mind, or the pill making me more emotionally needy. Maybe he wasn't special in any way at all. Was I making up stories in my head like my mother had?

After a few minutes I returned to the front room. I could smell the expectation in the air. He was standing by the easel again. What was going to happen next? I had no concrete plan of how to go about any of this. Perhaps I had naively hoped that whatever was about to happen would come naturally, with ease. The short distance between us was filled with a silence so loud it made my chest tight. It was as though I was faced with blank pages, and I didn't know what I was about to write. My heart was thudding hard.

I walked towards the sofas, and, as I did, so did he. We sat down, each on our own sofa. There was no way I could get him to leave now. He was staying. I could sense that.

'Silvia?'

'Mmm?'

'You say you haven't been colour-blind since birth. That's unusual. Very unusual…'

'Mmm.'

'I did a quick search online after we met. It's interesting. How did you lose your colour vision?'

I took a sip of tea, swirled the hot sweetness in my mouth, and counted three long deep breaths before I spoke. I lowered my voice; it felt safer that way.

'You have to understand, what I'm about to tell you… I don't know whether I should talk about it.'

I gave him one last long look to make sure that I trusted him – if this was the biggest mistake of my life, I at least had to make sure that in that moment I felt it was right. I did.

'It's just… I have to trust you,' I said.

The cup clinked against the small plate beneath it as my hands started to tremble. I put it down on the coffee table. 'Sorry,' I said.

He shook his head to let me know I had nothing to be sorry about.

'Uhm,' I tried to continue. I was fighting back tears, so I looked out of the window so that he wouldn't notice straight away. How embarrassing, I didn't want to cry in front of him. I took a deep breath and it helped. 'It's just, I've never actually told anyone this before, so maybe you should decide if that's a story you want to hear, and if you have time for that right now.'

He was silent.

'The point is, if I tell you this, it's a really big thing for me, so I need to make sure that you're definitely someone I want to tell. Because for some reason I suddenly feel like I want to tell you everything and I don't know why. I have no idea why.'

I suddenly felt embarrassed, and frightened. I was scared of what he would say. My heart was racing. I felt vulnerable. It took him a while to say anything.

'Well, I mean, only you can decide that. Only you can decide if I'm the person you want to tell it to. But if it helps, there's very little in this world that fazes me. I've experienced and seen many things. And I've also heard a hell of a lot of incredible stories. So I won't judge, if that's what you're worried about.'

Of course, I was dealing with an environmental human rights lawyer. And, on top of that, one who'd had a mind-blowing epiphany that flipped the meaning of his own life upside down.

Suddenly the world went still; everything slowed to a stop. My mouth went numb, as though it had been injected with anaesthetic. A little sound came out of it and then I was mute again. The room was so still and silent, and I felt that this was all a dream. I imagined myself running away. Running along a long empty road at the ocean's edge, the sun shining on me. A recurring dream I had. And I imagined it so vividly then, out of nowhere. The never-ending run. The never-ending escape – from the thoughts, the past, the memories, the lies, the prison, the pain. Ultimately, I longed to simply escape myself. To lose myself.

And yet, here I was, with this man, in this room, and my impulse to run was so abruptly succeeded by the most powerful desire to stay, to sink deeply into the moment. To not run. To not escape. To be here. To speak.

Luna

I was born on the night of a full moon. It was a large silver moon that lit up the night sky, and that's why my mother called me Silvia. Silver moon. But Luna was the nickname she gave me, and it became the name she most often used. *You're my little light in the night,* she'd say. *My light in the dark. My Luna.*

My mother, Alma, was originally from the city of Tromsø in Norway, but she went to live in London for her student years. She studied for a masters in applied ecology and conservation and spent a lot of time in Mexico, concentrating on forest conservation projects near and around Veracruz. That's where she first met my father.

My mother was an intelligent woman. She was like a walking encyclopaedia. But it wasn't just knowledge that she had – words, dates, figures and concepts – above all, I remember her for both her wisdom and her lack of it when it came to my father.

She was disillusioned with humanity. She'd spent years of her life studying theories of ecology, and the more she read, the more she became convinced of the absurdity of our species.

How had saving the planet even become an issue? How did it get to that? How had humans managed to become so removed in the first place? She used to say these things when she got particularly annoyed at something, and I used to shrug, because I was young and

I didn't understand what she meant. She used to talk to me a lot, because Diego, my dad, wasn't always there for her. And I used to go with her everywhere because there was no one else to look after me. She used to say to me that she felt stuck, that she didn't know how to make a difference. But she wanted to. She said, sometimes she felt the only way to make the proper urgent change that was needed would be through a radical revolution, a massive upheaval. *But it seems too confrontational,* she would say. *It's like fighting fire with fire.* Then she would add, *but maybe I only think like that because I'm from such a damn comfortable middle class background. I was taught to always be polite, to hold everything in, follow all the rules. And I could convince myself till eternity that we can fix all this without a massive confrontation, by just politely asking everyone to do the 'right thing'. Meanwhile the world is dying around me even more.* I'd shrug. *But you know Luna, sometimes I feel I just want to run away from all this, go live in the wilderness somewhere, and make my own food, live simply, sustain myself – that way I wouldn't be causing any more damage. And some say that's the way. But then I'd be removing myself from society and I wouldn't be able to influence change in a bigger way. But maybe it's not about that… Ay Luna, I just don't know!* And I didn't know either. I just listened to her, nodded, shrugged, and thought my mother was the cleverest and most beautiful mother in the world.

Sometimes, while she talked and talked, I would sit and draw her talking and talking. As her mouth opened and closed I sometimes imagined she was the little tweeting bird that sat outside my window and sung to me in the mornings.

The problem, for her, was that she felt powerless. Her life in Mexico restricted her, she would say. But did she leave Mexico to pursue those things she said she really wanted to do? No.

I don't know what I would do if I wasn't here Luna, but I don't think there's much potential for me here. I don't feel I can make much of an impact. I don't know what kind of dreams she had in her head, where it was that she imagined things would be different, and how they'd be different and what she would do. *Where* would things be better? I don't know if those dreams were ever properly formulated in her head, either. She'd probably feel just as unfulfilled anywhere else, and maybe deep down that's also what made her sad. But I think the biggest issue for her was that she felt like an outsider, she stuck out with her height, light ash blonde hair and blue eyes – how glad she was that I had been born with dark hair! She was the *gringa*, and maybe that frustrated her too. It made her self-conscious.

All I knew was that she loved Diego too much to ever leave. 'Love'. That word. I didn't understand it, what humans meant when they said it.

She worked for an environmental charity, but was unsatisfied with her job there – saying that she spent more time staring at pointless spreadsheets on a computer screen than actually making any kind of notable difference in the world. I used to imagine her head turning into a computer. On the side she worked on some translation projects to make ends meet, and to afford rare trips back to Norway to see her mother. My grandma was a woman of poor health who spent her last years in a hospice, and who was the only family my mother had left.

My mother was also deeply involved in local and national grassroots projects. For example, when an overseas company decided it could move into an apparently empty space without warning, clear land and mine for gold, or oil, she and her *compañeros* stood up to them. There were lots of different movements, and she made sure she was informed by as many of them as possible. Involving herself with these movements was, at the time, she said, one of the best things she felt she could do. It gave her a reason to travel around the country too, taking me with her. I remember she once whispered to me, *this is a beautiful country Luna*, as though it was our secret.

As time went by, she started to make a name for herself and gained the respect of locals and environmentalists from all over Mexico. And that in itself was a vital thing for her, and definitely contributed to her growing confidence. She didn't feel like just a *gringa* anymore.

Diego wasn't at all like my mother. Or at least I didn't see all of the wonderful things she saw in him. *You'd have to be me to understand*, she said. But I wasn't her, and I didn't understand. He was from Culiacán, in the state of Sinaloa, and I spent a lot of my early childhood round there. He knew people in the notorious local drug cartel and, to some, his involvement seemed a grey area. My mother kept well out of that world. I didn't know much about it either, I only heard rumours. And I didn't really know so much about my dad. I didn't see him that often. When I did he was drunk or high. I don't know exactly what happened or why but I know he hit her on more than one occasion. She blamed herself, saying she travelled around too much for his liking. But the truth was that *he* was around much less, and sometimes he didn't even tell us where he was going. I know that each time he went my mother wondered if he would come back. He'd hurt her and make her cry, and then she'd tell me she loved him. *It was different before*, said my mother. *Your dad's a good person Luna.* Was she trying to convince me or herself with those words? *He used to be different, but it doesn't matter, it doesn't change a thing, he's still a good person. He's had it tough, and sadness changes people.* Her words hurt me, because I knew she was hurting herself with them. She was lying to herself, and she believed her own lies. But love is blind.

I wanted never to be blind.

It used to be different, she said. But I'd never know what she meant by that.

Blindness

Alma: Sunday 9 August 1987

*I walk into this seedy little bar with two of my college friends and there he is,
that guy I saw at the talk the other day. I recognise those intense green eyes.
He's up front onstage, strumming his guitar, singing with a sexy soulful voice.
The warm light envelops him and beneath his shirt I see his muscles. Damn.
After half an hour and a drink Emelie and Maria want to move on – our
Scandinavian hair sticks out too much in this place and they look fed up with
engaging in polite conversation with the group of desperate men that's cornered
them. They don't seem to realise that I'm mesmerised.*

'He's amazing,' I whisper to Emelie, pointing at the stage.

*'Who? Diego?' She raises one perfectly shaped Swedish eyebrow, and I'm
shocked she knows his name. 'You're barking up the wrong tree my love… that
guy is crazy.'*

Crazy, eh? He sounds like someone I want to get to know.

*Three days later we're on our first proper date. We've ended up back at mine,
continuing our conversation with the extra help of marijuana. I'm in awe. I
didn't realise Diego was so radical. I feel like an impressionable ditsy teenager.
He's making me feel like a wannabe. He's a member of the* Frente ecológico,
a small group of eco-anarchists who are all about direct action. He actually goes

out and kicks ass, he shakes shit up on a regular basis. Earth liberation, as he calls it, is his life. He's my new idol. I can tell I'm going to learn a lot from him.

By the end of the night I think I'm in love.

Alma: Friday 15 September 1989

Diego is a strong guy, he's not someone to mess with. People look up to him. But they don't know him like I do. Behind closed doors, when I have him all to myself, I learn more and more about his vulnerabilities, and I can feel my love for him growing stronger. I want to take care of him; I want to protect him. I want to show him that everything is okay because we have each other. His mother died giving birth to him and his dad, wherever he is now, became an alcoholic. He's only close to one member of his family, his cousin Luis, because the rest of them – aunts, uncles and even grandparents – don't seem to care. Diego has had to fend for himself. It's made him more mature and determined than other guys I know. But it's also made him crave family.

The news of my pregnancy is met with a lot of celebration, I think this may just be the happiest I've ever been and the happiest I've ever seen Diego. As the day's celebrations come to a close and we're lying in bed, his body around mine, I drift off to sleep with a smile on my face. I think about how great a dad Diego will be and how happy he'll be to finally have the family he's craved.

Alma: Saturday 30 March 1991

Diego is playing with Silvia and I'm preparing dinner when the phone rings. I ask Diego if he can get it because my hands are covered in dough. I think I've added too much water to the tortilla mix, and I'm trying to fix it. Juan Flores' song Love and Pain *is playing on the radio and I'm humming and singing along…* Ooh sweet baby, I just can't figure it out… I just don't know if it's worth lovin' yooouuu… *when all of a sudden I hear a loud yell. It makes my blood curdle. I turn around and rush towards the phone. There I see*

Diego on his knees with tears streaming down his face. Silvia is sitting on the floor next to him staring blankly at her papa.

'Baby, what's wrong? What's wrong?' I ask him, clutching him by the shoulders, stroking his face, doing anything I can to let him know I am here for him, 'what's wrong? What's happened?'

He pushes me away and shakes his head. I reach for him again and again he pushes me away.

Diego's cousin has just died in the crossfire between two cartels. I have never seen anyone as sad and angry as Diego is now. I don't know how to comfort him, and he won't let me. I suddenly feel totally closed off from him.

Alma: Wednesday 23 October 1991

These days I walk around feeling anxious all the time. Diego keeps talking about revenge and I don't know how serious he is. It frightens me. I don't want to have anything to do with the cartels, and I beg him to not do anything stupid. Diego's abandoned his music, it's been months since he picked up his guitar, and he's rejecting invites to meetings with the Frente ecológico. I feel like he is slipping away from me. It's been a while since we made love. I guess I have to be patient and accept that this period of grieving will take a long time. I need to remain strong for him. I need to give love without expecting anything in return, no matter what. I need to be there for him, to take care of him, because soon things will be better again and we'll come out stronger for it.

I felt distracted at work today but now that I'm on my way home I'm feeling better. I plan to make us something special for dinner tonight, so I stop off at the grocery store to get some extra ingredients.

As I open our front door something doesn't feel right, I only realise seconds after that it's the smell of alcohol. Diego is sitting on a chair and resting his head on the kitchen table staring vacantly to the side. He doesn't blink, not even when I walk into his line of vision. A half empty bottle of vodka and a bag of cocaine are on the kitchen table. Silvia is crying in the other room. I register all these things in a split second and for a moment I think to myself my god he's dead. *But then I see him blink. I have to think fast. I don't know who to attend to first.*

'Diego! What the hell?!'

He sits up and stares in front of him. He doesn't look at me. Silvia's crying gets louder so I rush to the other room, pick her up and comfort her. Her nappy is drenched and stinks of shit. How long has she been lying alone and crying like this? My god. I cradle her in my arms, kiss her forehead and tell her hush, everything is okay.

I walk back into the kitchen, cradling Silvia close to me. I'm shaking with disbelief and anger. I'm starting to cry.

'Diego,' I say, 'what's going on?'

He turns to me now, and in a moment he too is crying. All my anger suddenly melts away and turns into pity. Oh god, my poor Diego. And we are all there by the kitchen table crying, hugging and comforting each other, and, though I am sad, I am grateful that he is letting me in again.

Later that night we make love and it is beautiful.

Alma: Tuesday 24 December 1991

It's Christmas Eve. Silvia is exactly nineteen months and fifteen days old today and as I look at her I contemplate how quickly time has passed. She's mucking around with crayons at one end of the kitchen table, while I'm on the other end, preparing Christmas dinner. I don't know where Diego is, but I told him to be back for six this evening.

It's already a quarter past and it's dark outside and I'm getting anxious. I know he's often late, but it's Christmas and I'd hoped he'd make the effort.

The door swings open and slams shut behind him. He's made it. My face lights up with a smile of relief. Hey sweetheart, Merry Christmas, *I say going to give him a kiss on the cheek.* Merry Christmas, *he says. But his head is somewhere completely different. I can't tell whether he's just distracted or on something.*

We eat our meal in silence. I think this is the worst Christmas I've ever had.

After I've tucked Silvia into bed I tiptoe into our room and shut the door behind me. Diego is sitting at the end of our bed. He gets up, embraces me and starts kissing me. His kisses feel urgent and now he's pressing my body against the bedroom door and I don't know if he realises how forceful he is being. He bites my lip. Hard. Suddenly he swings me round and pushes me onto the bed, face down. He's pinned me down and lifted my dress and is pulling off my underwear. He penetrates me from behind and I howl in pain. I struggle and try to fight him off. He turns me round so I'm face up, he slaps me in the face and he fucks me. He kisses and he bites and I can no longer respond. I can't move. I am numb.

He lands on top of me panting after he comes. I wait. His breathing finally slows to normal but I can feel he's starting to shake. He's crying.

'Oh god, Alma, I'm sorry, I'm so sorry...'

We're both crying.

I tell myself I don't believe in bad people, only people who've gone astray. All I want is for the Diego I once knew to come back, and for it to all be okay again.

The Forest

My mother's blind love for Diego taught me a valuable lesson: to keep away from love. Not that I had a choice. If I got close to someone I'd have to tell them everything, and then they too would have to live a life of secrecy and lies. I'd never want to do that to anyone, for the same reason I'd never want to have a child. Why bring a new life into this unkind world? Why bring a person into *my* insane world?

But the truth is that the concept humans have of love has confused me ever since I watched my mother's blindness. And then all the years that followed, all the lyrics of songs, films and books all confirmed how nonsensical this thing we called love was. My mother was an obvious case, of course. Most people think that, in the same position, they would be able to see that they were deluding themselves, but the truth is that most of the time the pain of love is far more subtle.

When people use the word 'love', they could just as easily replace it with 'need' or 'attachment' or 'addiction' – and I guess that becomes most obvious when people in one way or another lose that person they love. Then the suffering begins. The withdrawal. Then you see how painful it can be to have been attached to someone.

*

My mother and I travelled around a lot, and that's how I learned about the drug wars. I overheard people talking on the buses, and news would come on the radio. There was no way my mother could shield me from the truth of it. I thought the cartels were monsters. People were dying and disappearing all the time. I often thought that the monsters would come and get me too. Each month, each year seemed just as violent as the next. The US government was heavily involved in all of this of course. After all, 'the Mexicans' were responsible for supplying their country with the vast majority of illegal drugs. But the US also made out that their help would sort out Mexico's problems, all the drugs and violence. *Yes, that's right,* my mother would say, *the cherry on top is that they try to make us believe they're helping us out. What a load of bullshit.* It seemed we all knew the US government supplied the cartels with guns, and we'd heard many tales of how its agencies had laundered money for them. The US had no interest whatsoever in helping end the violence. Why would they? To them we were just another blur of *unpeople.*

It was around that time though that the US government made the decision to involve itself more heavily – 'time for a serious intervention,' they declared. Time to crack down on the evil drug lords and cartels once and for all.

*

Silvia: Friday 9 May 1997

Our forest is one of Mexico's most diverse cloud forests, *Mami says. It's my seventh birthday today, finally. I've been waiting a whole year for this day.*

Ahh, *says Mami,* time seems endless when you're little. It drags out from one birthday to the next. *But I don't understand what she means. Sometimes Mami says silly things. But I love her. Especially today, because she's taking me to the forest.*

When we're in the forest it makes me happy. It's beautiful. Mami talks to me about how climate change will affect the complex natural systems in these biodiverse cloud forests. *I don't know what she means and I don't like the sound of it, but I listen because I think maybe she will test me on this later. She says* drought could wipe out whole areas of forests. The ecological equilibrium of the ecosystems would be totally interrupted, and if the forests were lost it is supposed that at least a hundred and twenty species of vertebrates specific to that region would go extinct. *I frown because I've forgotten what half of those words mean, but I can't ask her because she's explained them to me millions of times and I don't want her to get angry. She looks at me with scary eyes and says* and that's just the vertebrates Luna! This could all happen within the space of only a few years!

Though I am still small, I am big enough to already know what some of those words mean and I know that Mami is talking about a lot of really bad news. As usual she is angry about it all, I can tell because of how her voice sounds funny when she speaks. But it is my birthday and I don't want her to be angry today. I wish she wasn't angry about things sometimes. Especially because the forest is really nice today and I think she should be happy instead. It's really really green and there's mist in the trees. I can hear birds going chirp chirp and insects going buzz buzz buzzzz, and I like to close my eyes sometimes and think that the forest is breathing. This is a magic forest. It makes me happy. But Mami's words and her angriness make me sad. I don't want to feel sad on my birthday.

But soon we are happy again! Mami has made me a surprise. She did a surprise birthday picnic with all my favourite things in it, which she put out on the big fluffy rainbow rug. There is chocolate cake, yummy avocado sandwiches, lemonade, corn tortillas, juicy salsas and salads, beans, spicy chilli chocolate cookies – my favourite! – and sweet potato fries… I eat and I eat and it tastes so good and Mami says I have a huge grin on my face and so does she and I am so happy!

The birds are singing so prettily and everything is green green green and we chat about all sorts of things and it is so good and perfect. Mami asks me what I want to be when I grow up, and I say a bird because it is true. She tells me about Norway and how the forests look different there. We talk and talk, and sometimes we go silent, just listening to the forest because it sounds nice and Mami thinks so too. And she doesn't even talk about Diego or talk about sad things or talk about how bad the world is because I think Mami is happy. This is the best birthday ever.

But after our picnic there is bad news with the forest. Mami says the cloud forest used to be way bigger than it was, and it had got lots smaller because of things like coffee and cattle growing on it and lots of new people coming to live in it with the native people. Lots of animals have already become extinct. Extinction is a bad thing. Mami says she would do anything for the forest to keep staying alive, and to not keep disappearing. And she says that if she could she would go back in time and make it not disappear from the start and not have all those animals get extinct, and make it like it was in the beginning because it was nicer in the beginning. I want to go back in time in a time machine too and see what the forest looked like a million years ago and see the animals that are now gone. I bet it was all really pretty.

Yes, Mami loves our forest. And everyone in the world knows that because she is getting famous because she is really clever and knows lots of people and lots of people know her and not just our neighbours but people from all over the whole wide world. Even far far away in England a really famous newspaper has written about Mami and her projects. The projects teach people how to save the planet and the animals and everything. I was there when she spoke to the newspaper man but she was speaking English and I didn't understand but I could see she was happy and I was happy too because Mami was getting famous. I made her a frame from sticks and glue and we framed the page from the famous English newspaper that she was in and we put it up in the kitchen for the whole wide world to see, but then it got moved into my room and I don't know why this happened but I think maybe Diego moved it because he didn't like it. He doesn't seem happy that people from all over the whole world know about Mami.

Silvia: Thursday 16 October 1997

Grandma in Norway has died and I'm so sad and I can't stop crying. I met her two times before and I really liked her and I don't understand why she had to die and why I will never get to see her again. It is horrible.

Now it is only me and Mami left in this world, because Diego doesn't count because I don't like him. But maybe it will all be okay in the end because I have Mami, and Mami is enough.

Alma: Tuesday 4 November 1997

I still can't believe she's gone. It wasn't a shock, but even so, there's a part of you that never quite wants to believe it will happen. I know I could have visited more. It took her own funeral to get me back to Norway for a visit. But I'm at peace. She left this world knowing that I'm okay. I suppose it's typical that only now she's not here I'm starting to really value all those words of kindness she showered on me after I sent her my article in The Guardian. *I did her proud and I'm glad about that, because if she'd left any earlier she'd have gone to the grave still worrying about me.*

I can't remember the last time I got to sit down like this at the table and drink a cup of coffee without having to be anywhere else, I've been so caught up in this crazy whirlwind. It's been one thing after the other. But good. It's about time someone listened.

Silvia's been adorable, more adorable than ever. She must think she has a celebrity for a mami. It's so good to see she's doing better now. With all that's been happening, I fear I haven't given her all the attention and comfort she needs. It's made me feel like a bad parent. God knows where Diego is. I sense Silvia's hate for him growing. My poor little Luna. But she looks happy now, drawing there in the corner. She's always in her happy place when she draws. Her right hand is covered in colourful pastel dust, as usual. My little genius. Who knows, maybe my baby girl will grow up to be a grande artiste.

A faint whoosh startles me and suddenly I'm staring at Pancho, the teenage son of one of my co-workers.

'Hey! What on earth are you doing? You can't just come flying in here unannounced. What's up?'

'Señora you have to come quick,' he pants.

'Why, what's wrong?'

'Señora... they've sold the forest.'

I drop my coffee. I don't even say goodbye to Silvia. I run.

*

The doorbell rang and Jack and I both jumped.

'Shit,' I said.

Max. It was six already.

'Oh my god,' I said, clasping my face in my hands. I suddenly registered that I was in the middle of the hardest and most honest conversation I'd ever had. A feeling of utter despair rushed through my body. *Oh my god, what have I done?*

'Silvia?' said Jack.

I was silent, I couldn't speak.

'Your dad... I'm so sorry to hear,' he was shaking his head.

The doorbell rang again.

I got up without looking at him.

'What happened to the forest?'

'I'm so sorry, you'll have to leave Jack.'

'Yes. Of course.' He got up.

My memory of Jack leaving and Max coming in is a blur, I don't even remember how that all panned out. I only remember desperately avoiding eye contact with both. For the next couple of hours I barely spoke. It was lucky that Max was used to me being hot and cold. I couldn't draw. Squiggles appeared on the paper but I was totally absent. I was a burning tangled mess of nerves. My head felt as though it would explode with adrenaline. I was terrified.

At eight o'clock, when I shut the door behind Max after saying a vacant goodbye, I ran to the kitchen, opened a cupboard, pulled out a bottle of wine and poured it down my throat, crying and spluttering as I gulped.

Why the fuck did I trust him?

I would have to tell him everything now.

Mountains

For days after Jack left my apartment he'd tried calling me and I didn't pick up. He texted me and I didn't reply. He wanted to see me and he wanted to know more. Could I blame him? We hadn't even got to the good bits of the story yet.

The taste of terror lingered in my mouth. I trusted him, but I couldn't help feeling as though somebody else knew what I was doing. I always felt like I was being watched.

By the fifth day I got tired of ignoring him. I was resigned. It was unavoidable now. I'd already gone too far.

I sat down and mulled over my options. If I was going to tell him everything I didn't want to do it at my apartment. And I didn't want to do it anywhere that anyone could overhear. I wanted to be away, far away, somewhere isolated.

I wanted to be in the mountains. In the mountains you can be alone, and you know when you are alone, because you can see all around. I hadn't been in the mountains for years.

Meet me at the entrance to the Paso Picacho campground at 11am on Tuesday. I finally sent him a text message. The Paso Picacho campground is the place to start for the Cuyamaca Peak hike. I'd never been before but, according to my research, it looked like a good place, and on a weekday the route was bound to be less crowded. We were more likely to be alone. I hoped my phone wasn't being tapped.

*

I thought I'd be waiting for him, but as the taxi pulled up I saw him, already there, waiting in the shade. I paid the driver, and as I opened the door was overwhelmed by the smell of pine.

'Hey,' I said.

I got my notes out – directions to the trailhead – and asked if he was happy for us to go for a walk.

'The Cuyamaca Peak?'

I nodded.

'Glad I'm wearing comfortable shoes.'

We walked to the trailhead in silence. We'd abandoned my notes because he already knew the way. It was a perfectly clear, warm summer's day and the smell of earth and wood felt so fresh. Light zapped through the trees and as branches swayed in the breeze, their shadows danced along the trail. Twigs crunched beneath our feet. A woodpecker drummed on a tree somewhere nearby. I asked myself why I hadn't been there before.

We engaged in a bit of small talk, which we both knew was utterly pointless and stupid. He asked me how I'd been, and hinted at the unanswered calls and messages. I turned to him.

'Look,' I whispered, even though there was no one around, 'do you have any idea how strange all this is for me? I should never have told you a thing.' Then I shut up because I didn't want to talk until we were out of the trees and I knew for absolute certain that we were alone. I told him this and he nodded. I think at that point he finally realised just how frightened I was.

After two hours hiking I finally felt like I was calming down. *He must think I'm insane.* I thought. *He must be wondering why on earth I've taken him all the way up here. And even I don't know the exact answer to that. Fear and paranoia primarily, but also a deep urge to get out of the city. A longing for open space and new horizons.* Perhaps it all sounds very poetic now, but I needed those mountains that day.

'Should we rest?' I pointed to a group of boulders a few metres off the trail.

'Sure.'

I looked around as we sat down. We were totally alone. We hadn't seen a single person for over an hour. It was almost eerie.

My lungs were full of new air and my head full of new perspective. High up there in those mountains I finally felt I had a voice. I was ready to speak. I was ready to let him in again.

*

Silvia: Tuesday 4 November 1997

I don't know who that naughty boy is and what he said when he came into our house like that without even knocking on our door but whatever it was Mami did not look happy. She spilled her coffee all over the table and now she is gone. I pick up my pastels and papers and I follow her because I want to know why she is gone and where she is going and what is happening but she is so much faster than me and I can barely keep up. She sees me and she says go back Silvia *but I don't go back because I want to be with her and I want to know what is happening.*

And now I'm tired of running and we are in a room that looks like a classroom except instead of children the room is full of all sorts of other people and I don't like it because I don't know anybody and I feel really small. It looks like people are serious and like everything is important, but I don't feel very important, and I don't want to make anyone angry so I go and I sit down in a corner and stay out of the way. I sit there for a really long time and more and more people are coming into the room and I am just waiting and wondering what is happening. Mami is talking one by one to everyone in the room but I don't want to go and ask her anything because I feel like if I do someone might get angry or trample on me.

Then the room goes silent and Mami and some other people are saying things at the front of the room and the other people are listening and they are sighing and I even see that there is a lady who is crying and then people start to talk louder and a man is shouting and there is a lot of angriness and sadness because the bad people are going to destroy our forest.

After a while I get tired of listening and the people's voices all merge into one hum hum hummm *and their heads turn into the squawking heads of birds. And there are some children and they turn into all sorts of animals, running around the room. And then there are some babies too and they are clinging to their mamis except they don't look like babies anymore because they are now sloths hanging from trees. And I can see a mist dancing around us all and I smile to myself as I fall asleep.*

Alma: Tuesday 4 November 1997

The biggest problem with the forest is that beneath the magical swirl of mist and birds, the canopy's orchestra of sounds and the rich damp soil that gives life to it all, there lives a reservoir of oil. For millions of years it's been there, living peacefully, secretly and undiscovered, and its existence has never been a problem. But now, they say, the forest is an unnecessary luxury. In the words of a close friend of certain US government officials, our forest has, up until now, been 'an unprofitable waste of space'. According to him it has a wealth of potential (what he actually means is a potential for wealth) and it should be exploited... by none other than his company.

No consultation is made with the people who live in the forest – neither by the oil company nor the Mexican government – who have signed away the forest so quickly and secretly that nobody even knew it was under threat. No information has been given about how much of the forest will be affected. In fact, nobody knows anything at all, except that it now belongs to someone, and that someone doesn't see the forest in quite the same way as we do.

Drilling will begin soon. If history is anything to go by, the indigenous communities living in the forest will be disregarded and removed. We discuss everything in our emergency meeting in the classroom: complex biodiverse ecosystems, the media, protest, compensation. I'm amazed at how many people have turned up at such short notice; it's a positive sign, but today is a sad day for us all.

As I walk back home with Silvia I feel grief-stricken. I'm already planning my next article. I have a title and an idea swirling round in my head. Mexico: The US's Back Garden *will be about our forest and the US's involvement in the environmental destruction of Mexico over the years. I'm going to send it to every newspaper here, in the US, the UK, all over the world. This story needs to reach an international audience.*

I am ready to fight.

*

And so my mother's devastation turned her into a woman of non-stop action. She was the busiest I had ever seen her. She would do anything for 'our forest', we all knew it. Even the governments knew it.

But how careful you have to be if the things you passionately care about are at odds with those with money and power.

The Colour Black

Alma: Friday 14 November 1997

I've done it. I've finally finished writing this damned article. I should have done this two weeks ago, when the news was fresh, but it's all been such chaos, there's been no time. If all goes to plan I may actually have some time to do other things today, like the laundry. Silvia's run out of clean socks. God, I've become a terrible mother these last couple of weeks. But she's an angel. She hasn't once complained, she just draws her days away, quietly content. Maybe I could make an extra special dinner for her today to try and make up for it. And read her some stories. Yes, she'd love that.

Diego came back this morning after four days of being god knows where. He was drunk again, of course.

He's sleeping in our room now, and he'll probably be there for the rest of the day. But I don't even want him to come out anymore. I want to be alone with Silvia. I need to spend some proper time with her, and I don't want to have to worry about him. I don't have time for that any more. I'm sick of this.

I take a sip of my coffee as I stare blankly at the computer screen. It's decided. I'm leaving him.

Silvia: Friday 14 November 1997

I am lying in bed, snuggled up to Mami and she smells like frangipani and is wearing that nice pink nighty and she is reading me Norwegian folktales about bears and snow and forests and trolls and giants and princesses with long long hair. Mami hasn't read to me in ages because she hasn't had any time since the forest got sold by the bad men so tonight she is making up for it with loads and loads of stories, and although I am sleepy I want to stay awake for as long as possible. I don't want to fall asleep but I can feel my eyes shutting and everything goes dark and I am floating off to the forests from the stories and riding on the back of a big white polar bear…

It is so beautiful…

Bang. *I sit up. What was that? Mami is sitting up next to me and the moon from outside the window shines on her wide-open eyes and she is breathing fast like she is scared. Then I hear footsteps, the door opens, the lights suddenly go on and there are two men with their faces covered in black.* Bang. *Mami falls back onto the pillow and blood comes out of her chest. Lots of it, quickly. And I know that Mami is dead.*

Everything goes black and I think maybe I am dead too and then I can see again but like on a black and white TV because there is no colour and even the blood is black now. The men are still here but everything is quiet except I can still hear the bang in my head. Everything is like slow motion and I think it must be a dream. Bright white doves creep out of Mami's chest, they spread their wings and flutter out of the open window and disappear into the night sky. No, this is a nightmare. *And then I feel wet on my leg and I look down and Mami's black blood is everywhere and I start to scream because this is not a dream.* Shut up, *says one of the men and he points his gun at me but the other man says* no *and pushes the gun away. He walks over to me and puts his hand on my mouth and it's cold and damp and it smells like metal and he picks me up and carries me away. I kick and I fight and then I can't move. I see Diego on the floor in the kitchen and he is not moving. All I can hear is my heart beating and this man breathing and everything is black and I am waiting to wake up.*

And then I wake up but I am in a car and everything is black and one man says what are we going to do with this little bitch? *And the other man says* she'll keep quiet, kids will believe anything, we'll tell her a story. *And then the other man says* well if she remembers our faces she's dead. *And then I wet myself. I am seven years old and I want to die.*

Playing Pretend

My smiling, shiny, artificial Argentine-American parents were lovely. Yes, lovely. *Good people*. Oscar and Flor Cruz, and their son Donny. Everyone loves *good people*. They cooked hearty food, they went to church every Sunday, they had many happy friends, and they were always smiling! Even at me! They said I was *such a great girl*.

How can I describe what it was like to live with them? It was like a prolonged, uncomfortable wait. A held breath. It was like those times when you go see your friend at their house, except your friend's not there yet, so you wait for them, and in the meantime you're stuck waiting around with their family. You put up with that discomfort though, because you know that soon enough you'll be with your friend, or you'll be able to go back home to your own family, and you'll be able to act natural again, to breathe. Except in my case, that held breath lasted eleven years. And there was no promise of a friend, a family member or any familiar face on the other side of that wait. But at least, after all those years, I could finally be alone. Finally I could breathe.

I don't remember the first couple of months with my new family very well because I was in bed, delirious. I was having constant nightmares about my parents' death.

But, during those first couple of months, the truth was that my artificial mother nursed me through my trauma with what seemed to be all the love of a real mother. My new family.

They only spoke to me in Spanish. I never went to school. *Home educated*, they called it. They taught me the usual: math, art, the US version of history, geography, religion, and all the other sorts of subjects you can generally expect to learn at school. We gave thanks to god at the dinner table. I played with them and their son for hours in the garden. We enjoyed the sunshine. We smiled and we laughed.

Officially, this family was doing a noble and compassionate thing. They had adopted a Mexican orphan – the innocent helpless victim of the terrible drug wars in that savage neighbouring country. Who could blame the poor child for having an evil drug lord for a dad? *Tut tut, poor child.*

As lovely and caring as my new family was, I was taught not to open up. The lesson to be learnt was that you can be a happy good Catholic without speaking your truth; you can still be lovely and smiley to people without letting them into your life too much.

And so now, homeschooled in rural California, lacking decent English language skills and having no real friends, I was not only half blind but also half mute. A muteness that sunk deep into my core.

Flor was a stay-at-home mother. She didn't go out to work like Oscar. It meant I never really had time to be completely alone.

I definitely didn't look like my new family. They were all blonde. It was a constant reminder of the past, a constant reminder of why I was different in the first place. Flor's hair was the fairest, a light gold. For the whole eleven years I was with them she always cut it the same length, just below her ears. Whenever I return to Flor in my memory I have a vision of her standing tall in the garden, her hair blowing a bit in the breeze, with the sunlight shining through it from behind and making her look like she has a halo. Maybe they tried to choose someone who looked a bit like my mother, but they didn't succeed. My mother was beautiful. Flor was average. Whilst Flor was confident and had a loud laugh, Oscar was quiet and temperamental. He had a big gut that hung over his belt. He wore thick-rimmed round glasses, which I always thought made him look stupid. I also have a go-to memory of him in the garden: he's digging because he wants to plant a birch tree he takes a quick pause to wipe drops of sweat off his forehead and to push his glasses up his nose. His breathing is heavy, his short-sleeved shirt has become too tight for him over the years, and he doesn't look fit enough for the job.

Sometimes we had a maid around too. Once we had a maid from Colombia. She was really nice to me. Her name was Lorena. I won't forget her because she was one of the first people I spoke to about my parents. It was just me and her that day. I was fifteen years old. She was the one who'd started to ask the questions, otherwise I would have never said a thing. The conversation started when she said *you don't look like your mama and papa*. I replied *they're not my mama and papa*. I told her that my parents had been killed because of Diego's involvement in the drug world. Diego killed on purpose, my mother by accident. Collateral damage. Those men who came in the night, who took away my mother and stripped my world of colour, they were just another weapon in the drug wars.

I remember she was so sad about what I told her, she actually started to cry. She asked me so many questions, as though she couldn't quite believe what had happened. I remember, when I went to bed that night it was the first time I started questioning the truth of my parents' death. In the months and years that followed, it slowly began to dawn on me that Diego would have never been on a cartel hit list. His level of involvement was as insignificant as thousands of others like him. However, Diego's shady dabblings and his dubious character – despised by even those closest to him as over the years his moral compass deteriorated – meant that he was the perfect decoy. I realised, finally, that those men had come for the sole purpose of executing my mother.

I never saw Lorena again after the day we spoke about my childhood. I started to wonder if we had cameras rigged in the house, or if she'd been fired after trying to talk to my new parents about it all. The roots of paranoia began to take hold.

*

I'm not in touch with the Cruz family anymore. I used to be, just after moving out, but never that often. I was too busy enjoying being alone. I had craved being alone for so long, I didn't even bother to try meet new people in that first year of freedom. And over the years that followed, as I faced up to the truth of why my mother was killed and why I had been given away to this fake family, I phased them out. It was surprisingly easy; after a while they gave up trying to stay in touch with me. I wondered if it had anything to do with Donny. I'm guessing they got distracted though, because the last time I saw them Flor was six months pregnant with twins. I don't know why she still wanted children at that age. She would have been almost fifty by then. It was an awkward meet up. We'd stuck to email contact for a long time before that, and the occasional phone call, but the contact got shorter and less frequent: the occasional *Happy Birthday* or *Merry Christmas* message, without questions and without an invite.

It was strange, I didn't know if Flor was the woman who'd looked after me when I was ill, tucked me into bed each night, and made me a birthday cake each year, or if she was the woman who, seventeen years ago, turned a blind eye to the truth, and agreed to feed me a lie. Of course she was both, but my head still refused to understand it. A huge part of me hated them for the lie they lived, and yet sometimes I'd get a flashback of something nice we once did as a family and I caught myself smiling.

And Donny, my fake brother, sometimes I still wondered about him. Though he was just under a year older than me, he didn't constitute a friend. Our relationship was strange and ultimately awkward. A true example of how you can feel lonely even in others' close company. But I had a lot of memories of him. I wondered what he was doing these days.

*

Silvia: Saturday 31 July 2004

It's Donny's fifteenth birthday today and he has some friends over and Flor and Oscar have made a barbecue in the garden. I haven't really met many of Donny's friends before, but there is this one boy, Josh, who I have definitely seen around. He looks like Brad from California Heights *on TV. I don't usually care much for boys, I think romance is stupid, but Josh is an exception because he is so hot. Anyway, I made sure I was wearing my favourite dress today.*

So we were all in the garden. The air smelled of smoke and cut grass. Me being me I didn't really talk to anyone, even though inside I was like oh my god Josh is so beautiful *and I was praying for there to be a moment where it was just me and him and he'd start talking to me and suddenly realise that I'm amazing, the most amazing person there. He'd tell me that actually he didn't really like Donny all that much and was just here for the free food. We'd laugh, talk, have a lot in common, and then we'd kiss! It would be a slow, romantic kiss. And then… then we'd run away together! Leave Donny and everyone behind!*

It's not that I hate Donny, I don't, but he's just not my real brother. Same with Oscar and Flor, they're okay, but sometimes I wish I could just run away.

Anyway, that never happened of course. I didn't talk to Josh. I've never even talked to a boy, apart from Donny. That's the other reason I want to run away. I never meet anyone. I don't have any friends of my own. I wish I went to school like normal kids. I want to meet people like they do on California Heights.

I was sitting on one of the chairs in the garden, and I was looking at the boys and thinking about Josh. They were all standing in a big group near the veranda and talking to each other and laughing and acting cool. Oscar was at the

87

barbecue, taking care of it and singing along to some old song that was playing on the radio. I think by this time he'd had quite a lot of wine 'cause his face was all sweaty and he looked pretty happy. I wanted to talk to Josh but that wasn't going to happen. I felt silly. I went inside the house to my room for a while and just lay on my bed feeling like a fool and wishing I was more confident. Flor came to check on me. I said I was okay. Just tired. She told me to come outside 'cause they were just about to do the cake. She waited for me while I went to the bathroom. And that's when I noticed it. I had started my period.

'Welcome to womanhood!' said Flor, when I plucked up the courage to tell her. 'I thought it would never come!' she said, because apparently fourteen was pretty late to start.

And although it was all so embarrassing I suddenly felt kind of excited. My boobs are finally gonna grow! Maybe then Josh will fancy me. Flor gave me a pack of maxi pads and she came to my room and looked in my wardrobe and handed me a dress.

'This one's red,' she said, 'so if anything happens it won't show.'

She left the room. I changed into the dress and looked at myself in the mirror. I've heard people say on TV that red is sexy. Although I can't see red I suddenly felt really sexy! And I walked out back into the garden feeling more confident than ever before because all of a sudden I was now a woman. And Donny was like how come you've changed? And all his friends turned round to look at me, and I said because I spilled coke on my dress, and he said oh and gave me this strange look, which I couldn't figure out.

Donny: Saturday 31 July 2004

It's my fifteenth birthday and we're having a barbecue. Mom and dad are not being overly embarrassing, which is good. Silvia's just come out of the house wearing a different dress. It's a red dress. Why has she changed? Johnny wolf whistles under his breath and the boys snigger. Your sister's hot, says Josh. She's not my sister and she's not hot, I say. Then I laugh because I suddenly feel awkward. They laugh with me. She doesn't seem to have noticed.

Books and Monsters

Jack had listened to my story, trying to suppress a look of horror, with the occasional tactful interjection. But now he was silent, just shaking his head and looking out at the horizon.

'Silvia?' he said at last.

'Yes?'

'How come they didn't kill you when they came for your parents?'

'I don't know Jack. I told you, I don't know.'

He wanted to know how exactly I'd found out the real reason my parents were killed. I didn't want to lie to him. It didn't feel right. But I felt that it wasn't necessary to tell him everything just yet. It didn't seem relevant. My answer wasn't a complete lie though. It was half true.

'Books,' I said.

When I was finally free to leave my artificial and fabricated family, I moved out. Not long after settling into my new place I fell in love with books. If I could give one piece of advice to politicians it would be this: you want a dumb nation? Close all the libraries and book shops.

You get a lot from reading, at least that's what I found. Because almost all books are about people: their lives, stories, experiences and all the details that go with them. And so, naturally, by reading other people's stories, I was drawn to my own. To the details.

At first I read children's storybooks. It was through the easy-reads that I taught myself to finally properly read English. Then all sorts of books. Historical fiction, romance, biographies, classic novels. The books helped me delve deep into my memories. For years I'd been taught to not ask questions, and finally something – perhaps inevitable – happened inside me, a light turned on.

I made sense of the world through books and art. Books I consumed and art I created. It wasn't necessarily a logical sense I was making of the world, but if nothing else the world certainly seemed less senseless when I read and when I created.

The money I received every month from the Cruz family was obscene. They were wealthy but even this seemed extravagant for them. At first I thought it was guilt money because they'd not fought hard enough to keep me when I moved out and drifted away from them. Then I started to think that maybe it was a compensation for the fact my mother got killed. Maybe it was filtering down from a higher power. I hadn't put all the dots together yet, and perhaps I didn't really want to. I had been taught for years to not ask too many questions, and I didn't want to overthink it. In fact, I didn't want to think about it at all.

I kept quiet. I kept myself to myself. I hadn't yet learned the art of communication. All those years with my fake family had been years of solitude of a strange kind. I'd been surrounded by people, and yet I'd felt utterly alone. Like there was a constant invisible and impenetrable barrier between me and them. No matter how close we appeared to get there was always a feeling of limit, of never fully being able to let go. I was my only friend. Why? Because I was terrified. My mind created monsters and I didn't know whether they were real or fantasy.

The monthly payments, and the simple fact I was still alive. It didn't add up. But the hardest part was the fear. The feeling that I was being observed. Perhaps I was wrong. Perhaps it was paranoia.

After all, it had been years, they should have forgotten about me by now. Perhaps. But it didn't stop the monsters in my mind. I was still running away from the bullet that I was spared from that night.

Who could I possibly turn to anyway? How can you run for help to the authorities when the authorities are probably the ones you're running away from? I kept my mouth shut so they'd have nothing to find. Nothing to see here. Just a normal life, a normal girl. I didn't want any trouble and I didn't want any more grief. I tried to give the appearance of living the most ordinary life I possibly could. Stay out of sight and out of mind.

I had enough money to not have to work. But I did work. I imagined it might keep me a little saner. Art was my distraction. The time I spent drawing, painting, sourcing art supplies, curating exhibitions, selling my work, all of that was time that kept me from thinking about other things. I don't know what I would have been like if I didn't have my art. I think I would have been even more of an outcast, more of a misfit. Maybe I'd have been drowning all the pain in alcohol and drugs on a daily basis, roaming the streets, maybe I'd be dead. All that time to think, I'm sure it would have killed me by now in some way. Maybe art was my drug, a drug that helped me to see the bright side, reminded me to focus on the beauty. And other times it was simple, pragmatic distraction.

*

The sun hid behind a cloud and a pleasant breeze blew over us. I stopped talking. There was probably more to say, but I felt I had come to some kind of close.

Could it be true that after all these years my story had been vocalised? Had I really just done this or was I asleep? Would I wake up and think *thank fuck that didn't actually happen!* Or would I think, *shit, that dream felt so good, I need to tell someone?*

It all felt so strange, I actually had to laugh.

Jack was silent, lost for words perhaps. I felt exhausted. I lay back on the boulder, stared up at the sky. A tear rolled down from the corner of my eye. I wiped it away quickly and closed my eyes and breathed deep.

'It's all so insane, isn't it?' I laughed. I was waiting for some kind of response or reaction.

'Silvia?'

'Yes?'

'Have you never thought to bring this forward to a lawyer, to someone who could help you?'

I laughed, but I didn't even answer him. The simple answer would have been yes, it had crossed my mind, but the fear of being found out had always been too strong. It was far easier to live by their rules of silence.

'Because you just did.'

Two Favours

Five days had passed since our last conversation. It was early afternoon and I was sitting at the kitchen table, waiting for the doorbell to ring.

'What could a lawyer possibly do for me?' I'd asked him. 'Those people who had my parents killed, they *are* the law. They make the rules. There is no escape.'

'You can't think like that,' he said. He was shocked and annoyed. 'Why do you think a job like mine even exists? Horrific things like this happen way more often that you can imagine. Who do you think is the biggest perpetrator of human rights and ecological violations? The giant corporations. The government. Its intelligence agencies. It's all tied up. It's all the same mechanism. It's because of that that my job has to even exist in the first place. I don't understand why you haven't done anything about any of this before.'

He sat there shaking his head as though he was disappointed in me. It made me angry.

'You just really don't get it, do you? They have all the power. They always win. What can anyone possibly do? It's like… we're tiny… and they're huge… it's impossible!'

'No,' he said, 'no, no, no. You just can't think like that. It's that kind of thought that gives them power.'

'I'm sorry Jack, but I don't believe you,' I said. 'I think you're being idealistic.'

He looked so offended.

'And *I* think you don't know enough about the work I do,' he said.

I wanted to believe him. I really wanted to believe him.

'Silvia,' he said, 'I'd like to take your case on.'

A thousand thoughts ran through my head and I didn't know which one to listen to. A case. *My case?*

'Jack, no one knows any of this except you. Don't you get it? Only you. And I'd like to keep it that way. I don't even know why I told you.'

'Look, listen to me – no one else needs to know about any of this until I have it figured out.'

I was shaking my head but I couldn't think of anything to say.

'You've been too scared to go to anyone all this time, haven't you? But you don't even know who you're afraid of in this situation!'

'Jack please, I really don't want to talk about this anymore.'

'I just want you to know that this is different.'

'What do you mean? What's different? What are you talking about?'

'Well, you didn't actively go and seek out some kind of help, did you? You're scared of having the responsibility in all of this. You were, understandably, scared of making that leap all by yourself.'

'I don't know…'

'Well this is different, because it's my decision, not yours. It's my responsibility, not yours. You can forget you ever told me any of this. Only when I come up with something will we revisit it, okay? In the meantime carry on living your secret life as you've always wanted.' He paused. 'But you haven't, have you?'

'Haven't what?'

'You didn't really think that you'd be able to live like this for the rest of your life, did you?'

It felt like he was interrogating me. Why was he suddenly so sure of all these things? He didn't know me.

'I… I don't know.'

'Silvia, you chose to tell me this for a reason. You made a decision to start finding out the truth.'

*

The doorbell rang at exactly 2pm. I'd needed a few days alone to calm down and to think.

'So this is what we do,' said Jack, once we'd sat down on the sofa. 'We stay put, you do things as usual, and in the meantime I'll start looking into things for you.'

'Thank you,' I said.

'No,' he said, 'don't thank me, I haven't done anything yet.'

'Well actually it looks like you have,' I said, fiddling about with a few documents he'd laid out on the coffee table.

'Look,' he said, 'think of it as a favour you're doing me. Some nutjob lawyers from my field spend their whole lives waiting or looking for a case like this. Seriously.'

He laughed and so did I – a little nervously perhaps, but I laughed. He was making me look at things in new light. I already felt more removed from everything that had happened to me, like a character from a film. Like I was watching a story unfold about someone else, not me. It felt good. It felt empowering.

'Okay,' he continued, 'so, we keep doing everything as normal, going about our business as usual, unless…' he stopped, 'unless something happens.' He paused again and looked me straight in the eyes. 'Any inkling,' he said, 'any inkling you get that something's changed, then you use this phone,' he said, looking down at the two phones he'd put on the coffee table. 'It's prepaid and you'll have to keep it charged, switched on and with you all the time.'

His face was stone serious. He handed me one of the phones

and slid the charger across the coffee table towards me. As I grasped the phone in my hand, my heart suddenly sunk. The realness of all of this was hitting me.

'And,' he continued, 'you send me a message, mine's the only number stored in it, and you say something trivial like, "See you at five on Thursday." What that message will mean is that as soon as I get it, we drop what we're doing, go home, get our bags and then we meet at the Westfield Horton Plaza Shopping Mall, and from there…' he paused, 'we hit the road.'

I burst out laughing and shook my head. Then I stopped. He was being serious. There was silence for a moment as we both contemplated those four last iconic words he'd said, and the actual reality that would come with them if his plan ever came to be. *We hit the road.*

'It has to be as soon as possible after the message is sent though,' he said breaking the silence with a hint of urgency. 'That's important. We don't want to be hanging around, because that's just too dodgy. It shouldn't take too long, right? To stop what we're doing, pick up our bags and get there? Right?'

He was looking at me. Fuck. He wanted an answer.

'I… I don't know,' I said. My mind was racing with all this information. He was speaking so fast, I could barely take all of it in.

'The Horton Plaza Westfield has a twenty-four hour gym, so whatever time we'd end up meeting wouldn't look strange. People go there at all kinds of times. So we meet outside the gym. Do you know it? Have you been to that mall?'

'Yeah,' I said, I'd been there just once before, 'it's the one with the kind of trippy buildings.'

'Yeah, that's the one.' He paused for a second as though he'd gotten sidetracked by his own thoughts. 'Good,' he continued, 'so whatever happens, don't take a lot with you, just a backpack or something, you know, something that could pass for a gym bag. And come dressed in gym wear.'

Suddenly a wave of dread hit me. This all seemed so uncomfortably real. It must have shown on my face.

'This is all just in case, don't forget,' he said.

'You… you told me it was unlikely.'

Just the other day he'd made me feel silly for my apparently overblown paranoia, saying it was unlikely anyone was still watching me, that anyone would find anything out. But now… now he was coming out with all this?

'Of course,' he said, 'of course it is. I'm just being hyper cautious, just in case. It's good to have a plan. Chances are no one is watching you or me at all, and to be honest that's the most likely scenario. I really don't think they are.'

He looked at me in a way that reassured me. I felt a little better. He had a way of suddenly changing his whole demeanour and with it making me feel immediately better. My body responded to his. It was strange, the weird way I had suddenly felt so relaxed when I first drew him. And surely he knew best. He was a lawyer after all.

'Text me tomorrow from your usual phone asking me if I'm free for another modelling session. Needless to say, make the text seem as normal as any you've ever sent.'

I nodded.

'We can discuss things further next time. I should go now,' he said, and he got up to leave.

We walked towards the door without looking at each other.

'Thank you,' I said, just before reaching the door.

'You need to stop saying that!' he smiled, 'Remember, we're both doing each other a favour.' And after a pause he quietly added, 'Pack your bags tonight and have them ready just in case. And start withdrawing as much cash as you can.'

'What? Really?'

'Yes.'

'Are we crazy?'

'Yes.' He smiled.

Knock Knock

I would have liked to have told him to stay and not to rush off that afternoon – but of course, I didn't. Instead I just agreed when he said he had to leave, and later regretted it. I wondered if somebody had tapped my phone. They'd already know Jack was a lawyer, because Pete had mentioned it when he called me on Thursday. But so what? So what if he was a lawyer? That didn't have to mean anything! And for fuck's sake, if anyone was somehow spying – and I didn't even know if they actually were, or ever had for that matter – how could they possibly ever keep track of all the people that came in and out of my daily life? It was absurd!

I had done as he'd told me that day. Half an hour after he'd left I went to the nearest cash point and I withdrew my limit of $800. I reminded myself that this was simply a precaution. Then I got home and packed my emergency bag, laughing to myself. Why was it now, when I was potentially less safe than before, that I felt so good? Why was it that something so serious felt like such a light-hearted joke all of a sudden? Maybe it was because all those years I'd kept a secret, and now I'd broken the chain and the secret didn't have its hold on me. Maybe now as I sifted through my wardrobe it felt as though I was packing for a vacation. It all felt quite absurd. I couldn't stop laughing. I picked up a wad of $750 from deep inside my underwear drawer – a cash payment from a painting I'd sold last month – and tossed it towards my bag. Then I grabbed another stash of $325 – the remainder of the funds I kept in the apartment to pay my models – and I threw it behind me, not even looking to see where it landed. More fits of laughter. There was something ridiculous about throwing all this money about; the adrenaline and this strange sense of joy. I put some uplifting dance music on and jumped, danced and even sung along while I chose what on earth would go into this bag of mine. I had never once felt quite as elated as this.

How could I pack this bag? I didn't even know where we would be going if we suddenly had to leave. I'd pack the bare essentials now and ask him later. One of the bare essentials – I'd already decided – was a small sketchpad. Wherever I went, I wanted to still be able to draw.

As I went to take a shower that night I stared at my reflection in the mirror and I suddenly felt nauseous. I threw up in the toilet bowl. That's when I realised how many nerves were hiding beneath this feeling of excitement I was experiencing. They had waited, skulking, surfacing in the night hours when everything seems worse.

Suddenly I was paralysed by a fear that I kept telling myself wasn't at all rational. I was so frightened. I felt scared to open the bathroom door because I feared whatever was behind it. I don't know what I imagined could have possibly been there. I feared that the monsters in my head were waiting for me in that room. I wished so much that Jack had never left me that afternoon.

I lay in bed, listening to every noise that interrupted the silence. Every far off footstep that echoed in the building, every gurgling pipe, every passing plane, nothing escaped my attention and it all seemed sinister. Each little sound made my heart beat faster. I was mad, I knew I was, but it didn't help to recognise it, it only made me more scared. At some point I finally fell asleep in a cold sweat.

*

Bang. I hear the gunshot. I see the blood. My world turns black. I am endlessly pulled back into this moment. I remember it in my dreams and in my waking hours. Sometimes the memory comes suddenly and violently out of nowhere and surprises me when I least expect it. So much time has passed and I still remember it so clearly. It's nagging me to find out the truth. It's like my mother won't leave me – she wants justice.

*

With daylight came sanity and a sense of great relief. I laughed at last night's fear and madness, at the half-packed bag on the chair near my bed and the crazy mess of clothes splayed around it. Before I knew it I was packing and repacking, as though getting it right was the most important thing in the world. After a while I had to abandon what I was doing as it was a little overwhelming and I found myself getting lost in something I thought was really unnecessary and daft. By now the bag was near full anyway, and even more clothes and toiletries surrounded it.

I made breakfast later than usual, having been distracted by packing. Then I made sure everything was prepared for the work I wanted to do in the afternoon. It was Monday and no one was coming over, it was just me, alone with my work, today, so really there was no schedule. Then I got dressed to go for a run. I rarely ran, but recently I was trying to get into it. It made me feel like a normal citizen of San Diego, and, above all, it actually made me feel good.

But at around 10am I heard knocking on my door. It startled me. I wasn't expecting anyone and no one ever usually knocked – people used the building's video intercom. I was paralysed. Last night's fears flooded back and took over me so quickly. The knocking continued. *Silly Silvia.* I shook my head. *How irrational.* But even so, when I walked towards the door, I did so on tiptoes, as quietly as I could.

'Silvia,' said a man's voice behind the door. A man's voice I swore I recognised.

I racked my brain for all the men I knew.

'Silvia de la Luz,' he said.

No one called me Silvia de la Luz. Not anymore. I always used my fake family's surname, Cruz. Silvia Cruz. No one could know my real surname unless they knew about my past. My heart was thudding so loud I was scared it would give me away. My hands went numb.

I caught a sudden glimpse of my reflection in a mirror on the wall, and it startled me so much I almost let out a cry. The blood had drained out of my face – the ghost of a girl in the mirror stared back at me. I felt sorry for her. I had never seen myself this lost and afraid.

'Silvia, I know you're home.'

Who knew I was home? Why?

Knock knock knock.

Thud thud thud.

'We need to talk.'

My god. That voice…

'We need to talk about what happened to your parents.'

A rush of adrenaline hit me. I grabbed the bag, rammed on my sneakers. I reached into the inner pocket of the bag and took out the phone Jack had given me. With my trembling fingers I tapped out: *See you at 5 on Thursday.* Send.

It wasn't far and I was ready. What if Jack was really far away? What if it took him ages to get there? I didn't want to wait around. Shit. I picked up the phone again. I thought. I racked my brain. What could I say? *It'll only take me about half an hour to get there*, I wrote. I tied up my hair into a tight bun, because it was something I never did and it made me look different. I picked up my keys and wallet, and took the sunglasses out of my bag. This was the best I could do to 'disguise' in the time I had.

By now the knocking had stopped. I waited a few more minutes, before looking through the peephole. Nobody there. I breathed some quiet deep breaths. Was Jack supposed to text me back? Or was less communication better in a situation like this? I really didn't know.

We'd never agreed on anything. But I had to go. I had to leave. *Now.* I went to the kitchen and put a small kitchen knife in my pocket.

I stalked down the corridor with my head down. The previous evening I'd thought to check for a rear exit to this building. Just yesterday my half-hearted preparations for a possible escape with Jack had been a game I was playing. A fantasy. I hadn't imagined that so quickly it would become real. The same never-ending concrete staircase I'd wandered down yesterday, I ran down today, legs like jelly. I had eighteen floors to get down. As soon as I got to the bottom, I'd be greeted by a wide door, which led out onto a quiet courtyard with a short narrow passage that led out onto the road. I would put my sunglasses on, blend into the crowd, walk a few blocks away, get a taxi and get the fuck away from here. My heart was drumming and my legs felt as though they were ready to collapse beneath me as I stepped down from the last stair and reached the door. *Finally. Legs, don't fail me now. Keep going Silvia, keep going.* I took a deep breath as I placed my hand on the door's handle. I was trembling all over. *Come on Silvia, it's okay.* I tried to calm myself. *You're safer out there than in here. Come on.* Finally I pressed down on the handle and pushed. Fuck. Nothing. *Fuck.* It was locked. *No, Silvia, no, you can't cry now. Go go, keep going!* I considered my options and then decided I really only had one. I started marching back up the stairs. On my way I tried to compose myself. *No tears. Breathe. You're normal. Everything is normal. Act normal. You'll be fine.* I tried to avoid my thoughts as best I could. After climbing three flights I walked through a door that led out onto one of the lower floors of the building. I walked along the carpeted corridors, passing the numbered doors of different apartments, and trying to find my way to the lift. I was walking as quietly as I could, listening out for any sounds, any clues that someone might be around. I found the lift. I pressed the button repeatedly. The lift came. Down I went. *Don't think Silvia,* I told myself again as I felt my heart race out of control as the lift travelled down. *Just don't think*. I closed my eyes and everything felt like it was in slow motion. The lift came to a halt as it reached the ground floor. *Ping*. I opened my eyes wide and I braced myself. The doors slid open. My heart stopped and I held my breath. I looked. No one. Nothing. Just the comforting sound of city life outside the foyer. I took a couple of steps forward and for a few seconds I just stood there as though I had forgotten everything that was happening. I was alone, totally alone. The lift doors closed behind me and the sound spurred me back into action. *Better out there than in here,* I repeated to myself once again. I emptied my mailbox and shoved the contents into my bag. *Go, just fucking go! Get out of here now!* I put on my sunglasses and I left.

At the mall I waited outside the gym, as Jack had instructed. I tried my best to look relaxed, as though I was casually waiting for someone. I only waited fifteen minutes, but it felt like hours. All the while I fiddled with the phone, praying he'd definitely received my text. A white, old-looking Chevrolet van with a surfboard strapped to the roof approached. Jack was behind the wheel. Relief. So much relief I almost smiled. I opened the door and climbed in. He looked at me briefly and started driving before saying anything. He was waiting for me to explain what the hell was going on.

The words didn't come out, my voice started trembling and I started to cry, as I felt I could finally release the pent up nerves. I wiped the tears away with my sleeve. Fuck, I was crying in front of him. I never cried in front of anyone. I felt so stupid.

'Sorry,' I said, 'I'm fucking scared.'

For a few minutes we said nothing. Absolutely nothing.

'So are you going to tell me what happened?' he finally said.

'Someone knocked on my door.'

He was waiting for me to elaborate, but in that moment I really didn't want to relive what had happened.

'Someone knocked on your door?! What the hell's that supposed to mean?'

'Give me a second,' I said, 'I'm sorry I just need a bit of time to process stuff in my head.'

For a long time after I'd told him what had happened he kept repeating the same questions to me: Could the man who'd knocked on my door been someone else? Someone who wasn't a threat? Someone perhaps who I knew from my childhood but had forgotten about? My answer was of course no. There could be no one. Of that I was totally sure.

'But if they knew you were inside, they would have surely waited for you to come out?' Jack said. He couldn't comprehend why anyone would so openly mention the possibility of talking about my parents.

'And why are they suddenly after you? How could they have possibly found out you'd told someone in such a short space of time?'

I don't know. I thought he'd know more about these things than me. But he was baffled by it, and that scared the shit out of me. I wanted to be as far away from the apartment as possible.

Out of habit I went to reach for my phone to check the time.

'Shit.'

'What?' he said.

'I think I left my phone behind in the apartment.'

'Which one? The one I gave you?'

'No, I have that one,' I said, still checking through my bag and pockets. 'It's the other one. My one. I don't have it.'

'Is that a problem?' he asked.

'Well… I mean… I suppose… I don't know. Is it?'

'Well you won't exactly be needing it now, will you? You know, it's probably best you didn't take that phone,' he said. 'You can track phones all too easily these days.'

God. We were actually running away, weren't we?

'How long did it take you to get to the gym anyway?' I asked, after a long silence, trying to appease my nervousness with an alternative conversation.

'Not long at all actually,' he said, sounding quite cheery all of a sudden, 'it's crazy. I was at my friend's house. Remember Adam, the one I told you about?'

I couldn't remember but made out that I did.

'He lives just a few blocks from the Horton Plaza,' he continued.

I looked back at the van full of cardboard boxes and all sorts of stuff.

'So how did you…?'

'Yeah, that's the crazy part. After last night I went home and prepared stuff, you know, just in case…' he sounded embarrassed. 'I mean I just thought I'd get it done and out of the way straight away.'

I wondered about his enthusiasm. Yesterday this was all just a hypothetical emergency plan.

'It took a while, because of all the books and documents I wanted to get together for your case.'

Every time he said the word *case* I felt a small hint of excitement in my stomach, a miniscule flutter of butterflies, barely perceptible. A small sense of hope, I guess.

'After all the packing I couldn't sleep, so I called Adam and drove over to his.'

'With all of this?' I asked, pointing to the back of the van.

'Yes,' he nodded.

'And he's a good friend?'

I was starting to wonder how much Adam knew. Jack must have sensed that.

'Yes, he's a really good friend. A really, really good one,' he looked at me for a second, 'and don't worry,' he said, 'he doesn't know who you are and he doesn't know any of the details of your case. But he knows you exist. I thought it only safe to at least have someone know something before I left.'

I nodded slowly, looking out at the car in front of us. For a second I again wondered what I was getting myself into.

'Okay,' I said.

'He's a lawyer too. Same field as me. We used to study together. Me and Adam… we've been through a lot.'

He stopped, as though he didn't want to go into any more details. We were silent for a moment.

'So did you actually think this day was definitely going to come? You had me convinced it was just a precaution.'

'I had no idea,' he said finally.

I glanced back into the van again. There was a wetsuit and a towel strewn across a couple of boxes. It almost looked like one man's idea of a summer vacation. And then I remembered there was a surfboard strapped to the roof.

'And what's the surfboard for? Do you plan to go surfing or something, while I sit around wondering if I'm going to be kidnapped?' Who was this guy I had decided to trust with my life?

'Oh no, I don't surf. That's one of Adam's… it's just a last minute touch, something to make us look less suspect. I'll take it off the roof and put it in the back when we're up north.'

'Oh really? How far north? Where are we even going?'

I felt so clueless about this whole plan. He was quiet for a while, as though he was thinking about how to formulate his words.

'Have you ever been to Alaska?' he said.

'Alaska?!'

'Yes. Have you ever been?'

'No, of course not.'

'No, well neither have I,' he paused, 'but I'd like to.'

'Oh, so this *is* some kind of vacation for you?!'

He didn't respond. He just looked on at the road ahead.

'We're going to Alaska?' I said.

'Yes,' he laughed.

'Are you serious? You're fucking crazy!' I said, 'and what about the borders?' I asked. If there was any chance that the authorities were looking for us, there was no way we'd ever be able to pass through any border controls.

'Don't worry,' he said, 'I have a way.'

I looked out of my window, wide-eyed, trying to comprehend the magnitude of all that was happening. What the fuck had I agreed to? Who was this guy? Was he actually serious?

'I haven't packed enough stuff,' I mumbled, more to myself than to him.

'That's okay,' he said, 'I have enough for the both of us.'

'And do I get any say in this?' I asked, still looking out of my window.

'Not really.'

I looked at him. The thing is, strangely, my lack of control or understanding in this situation didn't seem to bother me. For some reason, I'd decided from the start that I trusted him. Whether I was right or wrong to feel that way I didn't know. Maybe it was ludicrous and maybe it was insane but it was that inexplicable and almost incomprehensible sense of trust I felt for this stranger that had made me tell him everything in the first place. And so now I had to take another leap of faith and trust in his plan too, even if it meant going all the way to Alaska with him.

Jesus. Alaska. It seemed totally absurd.

But whether I actually trusted his plan or not there was little else I could do but stay in that van with him for the time being.

I took him up on all of this because I had nothing to lose. Really, nothing. I don't know what I'd expected would ever come of this life of mine. Perhaps more years of rolling along alone, never letting anyone in. Only now, I realised I'd always wanted to run away. And maybe he'd suggested the whole thing because he too had nothing to lose. Maybe we'd both actually secretly wanted an excuse to hit the road, break away and start something new. We were mad.

I sunk into the seat, got comfortable and watched the streets, buildings and people of the outskirts of San Diego zoom past outside the van.

'And so are there things I can and can't ask you about this plan of yours?' I said.

'You can ask me anything at all. I'm not keeping any secrets from you.'

'Okay. Good.'

I sunk even deeper into the chair, leaned my head on my window and looked out at the sky.

He laughed. 'Who said anything about a plan though?'

First Stop

'This is stunning,' I said.

'Yeah.'

'Apart from the other day at Cuyamaca, I haven't been outside the city for years.'

'Wow. Really?'

'Yeah, I swear it's been like over five years or something.'

'That's crazy.'

We were quiet for a while, just staring at the view.

'This is nothing,' he said, 'not compared to the other stuff we'll see on this trip.'

'This really is like a vacation for you, isn't it? Some kind of adventure or something.'

He shrugged and shook his head, but didn't say anything. It was as though he was keeping something from me. I thought for a while, trying to understand him and see where he was coming from in all of this. Why he was doing any of it?

'Hey,' I said, 'it's not like that's a bad thing. I could do with a vacation too.' I smiled.

'Do you go to the sea much?'

'Sometimes. But the beaches round San Diego can get kinda crowded... it's not the same.'

'Yes... true... but even so, just to see the sea, you know? There's something about it. There's a hell of a lot of beautiful spots up the Californian coast, but I guess it makes it easier if you have a car.'

I nodded. 'I suppose we'll be seeing them, then?'

'No. I've pretty much seen most of the coast. Been there. Done that,' he laughed. 'Time to explore inland. I want to see something new.' He searched my face for a reaction. He wanted to know if I was taking him seriously or not. 'You know... a new *adventure*.'

We continued looking out at the space before us in silence. For me this really was something else. I'd forgotten all about the existence of the natural world. Except, it turned out, that this was a manmade reservoir. It didn't look artificial at all – it looked like a real huge natural lake, and the mountains that surrounded it – the San Bernardinos – were breathtakingly beautiful. The air smelled of warm dry earth and the breeze felt like summer. Being there brought back memories and sensations from the past. Good ones. There was something quite purifying about it. A release. I felt a sense of liberation.

'This,' I said, pointing at the view, 'really is quite something for me.'

'I can imagine,' he said, 'I don't know how you've managed without it all this time.'

When we got back to the van I felt blissed out. It was almost embarrassing. All I seemed capable of doing was staring into space in silence with a half smile on my face.

'You okay?' he said.

'Yeah, I'm just suddenly really... really...' I searched for the word, 'relaxed.'

He laughed.

'It's stupid, I know. It's just, it's been a while. Shit, I feel like I'm high or something,' I said, and I laughed.

'No, it's good. I get it,' he said, 'I totally get it. I get like that often.'

There was silence as we both stared out of the windscreen. I hesitated.

'A joint right now wouldn't go amiss though,' I said, trying to suss him out a little more. Weed was fine, everyone smoked weed, right? Besides, hadn't he mentioned something about a friend of his who was into psychedelics or something?

He turned round, looked me straight in the eyes and smiled. 'No, it wouldn't,' he said. Again he turned round to look out of the windscreen. 'The problem is,' he said, 'I didn't pack any.'

'That's okay,' I said, 'I did.'

We laughed. I think this made us both realise that we still didn't actually know each other at all.

'I have something else though,' he said. He didn't look at me, and he looked as though he was hesitating. 'You don't have to be a part of it,' he continued, 'but since we're on the subject, I thought I'd share…'

'Oh yeah? What is it?'

'Adam gave it to me, because well… you know I told you about the thing… that time on the beach in Montauk?'

'Uh-huh…'

'Well, have you ever read *The Doors of Perception*? Aldous Huxley?'

'No.'

'Okay. Well I only just read it recently. Adam gave it to me because he thought I might find it interesting…'

'So… what is it?'

'Well in that book Huxley talks all about how he experiences things during a mescaline trip and—'

'Mescaline?'

'Yes.'

'You're crazy!' I said, and yet I found myself smiling.

He smiled back but said nothing. I shook my head and I looked at this guy and I suddenly felt awe and bewilderment at all that was presently happening. Who was he? I really had no idea.

'Mescaline,' I said again, 'Interesting.'

'Mmm. I mean I don't know if I'll definitely try it or not…'

'Why not?'

'Well the thing is… the book is interesting. There's a lot of discussion about our visual perception and colour,' he paused for a second and I knew why.

'Really Jack, you don't have to feel bad talking about colour in front of me. Please!'

'Yes, sorry, that's stupid of me.'

'Anyway, go on,' I said.

'Well, he talks about perception. How when we see things, we see them through the filter of our mind. We don't see things for what they are but for what we think they are.'

'Like the stuff you were talking about at Balboa, right?'

'Yes. Absolutely,' he said. 'But then, in terms of the realisation I had on the beach, it seems like the mescaline trip wouldn't quite cut it, at least not according to Huxley's write up of it. It made me think,' he said, 'maybe the trip will be a disappointment. Or maybe it won't. But in any case, why should I need mescaline to make me reconnect with that moment of clarity? Perhaps the only reason I can't feel it now is because I'm looking for it. Like a fish swimming in the sea wondering what water is and how he can find it.'

I laughed. 'Well, it kind of sounds like you're beating yourself up about it,' I said. 'If it's like you say, if nothing matters, if all is well and life is just one big divine fucking joke then there's really nothing stopping you from trying it, right?'

'True.'

'Sounds to me like you're making it out to be some kind of really important, meaningful and serious decision. But if nothing matters then who gives a shit. Do it or don't do it. It doesn't matter either way.'

He was looking right at me, grinning.

'Damn,' he said, 'I like you.'

I shrugged, but my ego secretly lapped up his words.

'Anyway,' I said, 'it sounds to me like you want to try it.'

'It does?'

'Sure. You wouldn't have brought it along otherwise… and you certainly wouldn't be telling me about it.'

The truth is, I was kind of putting words in his mouth. I wanted to try it. If there was anything at all that could help me see the world more clearly, the way he described it, the way I remembered seeing it as a child, I wanted to try it. If we were really going to see more of these beautiful landscapes, like he'd suggested, then I wanted to see them with the eyes of that child.

'I'd be happy to try it with you sometime if you like…'

I tried to sound casual about it. He didn't say anything but nodded to show that he was, if nothing else, acknowledging what I'd said. He ignited the engine and we drove off in silence.

Lakes

As we drove on, I watched the views outside and they were beautiful, but I didn't feel that same sense of bliss and freedom I'd felt at our first stop. My fear was back and deeply rooted. I sat slumped – tucked into my seat as though somehow that would better hide me. I put on my sunglasses and I eyed all the cars around us suspiciously. Then I eyed a pair of scissors that were lying on the dashboard. I had been toying with an idea for quite a while now, and I finally decided to share it with him.

'Jack, I think I need to change my hair.'

Silence.

'I mean like cut it or dye it. You know. Just in case,' I said.

Again, silence.

'What do you think?' I said.

'I don't know,' he said at last, sounding worried.

'You don't think it'd be safer to do that?'

He shrugged. 'Maybe.'

*

After an hour or so I suddenly noticed a dark Ford in my side view mirror. The man behind the wheel was wearing sunglasses and a suit. My heart started beating fast. I told Jack, and he said that the car had been right behind us for the best part of an hour. My god. Jack tried to calm me down, but it didn't work. I could tell he was glancing in his rearview mirror more frequently. The man in the Ford opened his mouth, said something and then smiled. He did a quick glance to the back seat. A little arm appeared from the back seat and handed him what looked like a soft toy.

'Oh my god, thank fuck,' I said.

I breathed a sigh of relief, and if I wasn't mistaken Jack breathed it with me. The car soon turned off the highway. If I'd have noticed the man and the car from the start, when Jack first had, I don't know what I would have done.

After a few more hours on the road we drove through Bishop, then took a quick break at a gas station to use the toilets. Jack went off to get a few things while I stayed in the van. I felt safer there. I asked him to get me blonde hair dye. He laughed, but when he returned he handed me a small shopping bag with something inside. I pulled out a box of hair dye. On it was an image of a model that looked like she was having outrageous fun with her blonde hair and her life in general. How ironic.

Jack said he wasn't sure it was necessary. He said that if anyone was looking for us they'd have better ways of finding us than searching out women with long dark hair. I put the box of hair dye away and decided not to think about it for now.

An hour later and we were at a lake.

'Mono Lake,' Jack said, as he trailed off the road and stopped the van.

'It's pretty.'

'I'm going to go for a swim.'

'You're what?'

'I'm going for a swim. You should join me.'

'Are you serious? Shouldn't we keep driving?'

'I need a break.'

He started driving again. 'I'll park way out over there. Don't worry, we're totally safe,' he said.

'Jack. Are you out of your mind? We need to keep driving.'

He didn't say anything. I closed my eyes and breathed deep. I tried to remember how I'd felt when I first met him, how unusually calm he'd made me feel. How I felt when we made that first stop and I'd breathed in the golden smell off the mountains around us. I told myself that if I'd trusted him up to this point, I had to trust him now. But even so, despite his efforts to coax me out and get me to go for a swim, I stayed put in the van.

'You'll have to come out at some point,' he said.

I watched him as he walked to the water, half naked and holding his camera. And I watched him as he swam and I felt pangs of jealousy.

Later, when he returned, he was grinning like a kid. It was already dusk when he was drying himself off. He looked out towards the lake and told me about how beautiful the pinks and purples in the sky were.

I liked it when people described the colours of things to me. It was rare – of the few people I spent time with, most didn't know I was colour blind.

Jack hesitated and then he said, 'Look, let me show you something.' He fiddled with his camera and then paced closer towards me and extended his arm, showing me what was on the small screen on the back of the camera. It was an underwater photo. Rays of light pierced through the surface of the water, and, beneath, some murky formation could be seen.

'Did you take that just now?'

'Yes.'

'It's pretty. Bet the colours are beautiful.'

'It's black and white,' he said. 'I guess it's closer to how you'd see it if you went under?'

I took the camera into my own hands and stared at the photo a little longer. I was fascinated by the fact that there was something that looked the same to me as it did to Jack. It was as though in some way he was melting away a divide between us. I looked up at him, handed the camera back and attempted a smile.

'It's getting dark,' he said, 'we should find a place to park up and sleep.'

'Aren't we gonna carry on driving?'

'No, we'll drive more tomorrow, we've been on the road for nine hours, and, to be honest, I'm a little drained.'

I didn't say anything.

'Look, don't worry,' he said, 'we're safe round these areas. No one's going to think to look out here.' And after a pause he added, 'besides, you won't regret it. Yosemite is beautiful. You'll see.'

Again I said nothing. I was annoyed. How could he be so calm?

We drove round to the east shore of the lake via a very basic sandy track.

When he finally found a nook he was satisfied with, Jack stopped the van and started rummaging through his backpack.

'So is this where we're going to sleep?' I said.

'Yes.'

He showed me how to recline the front seat.

'I don't like the idea of sleeping next to this window.'

I had visions of 'them' finding us and watching me while I slept.

'Well maybe you can sleep in the back. You can draw the curtains there.'

And that's where I slept. He cleared a space and lay out some rugs and, alone in the back, after double-checking that all the doors were locked, I drifted off into a world of terrifying dreams.

*

The next day I woke up surprisingly late, but despite the bad sleep, I felt better, less anxious. Perhaps it was because I was relieved to wake up from my nightmares and realise they were just dreams. Because, although I had so much to fear in the waking hours, the scenery that surrounded us was breathtaking, and all the fears seemed almost unreal that morning. I didn't mind Jack taking another swim in the lake, I didn't mind that we stayed there to eat, and I didn't mind that later on he stopped at Lake Tahoe for another swim.

Again he couldn't convince me to go for a swim, but I did leave the van to sit in the sunshine. There were only a few families nearby. I liked being around families. No one was going to kill me in front of a family. After muttering something about taking care in the sun, Jack left me and headed towards the lake. I had noticed that he often avoided the sun despite saying he loved it. I really did love it, and always had. It gave me life. Besides, my skin wasn't pale like his, I rarely got burnt.

Lake Tahoe was stunning, and under different circumstances I would have loved to walk around its shores. I yearned to explore the area and lose myself in it. Yosemite really was beautiful and I couldn't forgive myself for never having ventured out of the city alone. I was a strange girl. What had I been doing with my life all that time? Whiling away the hours, days, months and years. And what would happen to my life now?

As I sat, I drew. I wasn't used to drawing natural landscapes. My mind and hand found it hard to adjust to these non-human forms. I wasn't satisfied with my attempts and I quickly became frustrated. I put my sketchpad down and gave up. *Fuck it.* I got up and went to get the scissors from the van. I hid behind the van and carefully chopped great long chunks of my hair off. I didn't give a shit anymore, and it felt liberating. I only cut it to my shoulders, but even so, it felt like a big change. When Jack got back and noticed my hair, all he did was smile and say, 'Good, I'm glad you didn't chop it all off.'

The Shack

We stopped to freshen up at a gas station. It was by no means a pleasant experience. The tight white tiled cubicle with its depressingly bright light and cloudy scratched mirror stunk of piss and bleach, and I felt like even the water running from the tap was dirty. But even so, taking the time to brush my teeth, change my underwear and wash myself had the effect of making me feel more human. I struggled to fill up a big five litre plastic bottle with tap water in the small sink. Fifteen minutes later I left the cubicle spluttering – I had gotten a little excessive with my aerosol deodorant in a desperate attempt to feel clean and normal again. A woman was standing outside and she looked pissed off for having had to wait so long. She pushed past me and slammed the toilet door behind her. *Jeez*.

I looked around. Jack was already at the van. Good. I wouldn't have wanted to wait around for him in a place like this. There were more people round here and they didn't all look like happy vacationers. I didn't feel as safe in places like this as I had near the lakes and mountains. Jack was holding a folded newspaper in his hands and reading it as I approached him. He caught sight of me.

'Hey,' he said, 'I just need to go back and get a few more things, won't be a sec.'

I waited in the van impatiently. A couple of minutes later he was back with a bag of shopping that looked heavy, and he was still holding that newspaper in his hand. He climbed into the van and put the shopping bag behind his seat with a hefty clunk. I waited for him to start the engine but for a moment he just sat there, silently, not really doing anything. I waited.

'So,' he finally said, 'when was the last time you saw a live band?'

Oh god, was this another thing for me to feel embarrassed about? Just like the fact I hadn't been out of the city for so long? I looked him in the eyes, quickly trying to suss out what his reaction might be.

'A very, very long time.'

He raised his eyebrows.

'Really?' he said.

A sudden wave of anger soared through my body and I lashed out at him before I could stop myself.

'Is that really so fucking incomprehensible to you? What, have you already forgotten that I haven't exactly been living a fun, free, normal fucking life?'

He didn't say anything. We were both silent. The sound of my raised voice left an unpleasant ringing in my ears. He started the engine, the radio came on and we drove off. I turned my body, leaned back in my seat, looked out of my window and pretended to be asleep while I secretly cried.

*

Beer had been a good idea; it relaxed me. It was dark and we were parked amongst other cars and trucks in the dirt outside the little building with the neon sign that read *The Shack*. After I had calmed down I had given in to his idea to come. I also told him he was crazy, and that I had no idea why I had ever trusted him in the first place, when he was clearly treating all of this like an excuse for a fun summer vacation. But I mellowed out after a small joint and a beer. We were waiting for more people to arrive, Jack didn't think it mattered, but I was scared that unless it was rammed in there we'd stick out. I picked up the newspaper from the dashboard and glanced over the description again: 'Monthly Jams at The Shack'. Every now and then, when someone flung the doors open to either enter or leave, I could hear music and bass-lines. There were groups of people hanging out outside drinking, smoking, laughing. They seemed friendly. The more beer I drank the more the music sounded inviting.

'Come on,' he said, 'let's go in.'

I nodded.

'Tonight Silvia, we're forgetting everything. Everything. We're having some fun.'

I rolled my eyes. *God help me.* I downed the rest of the beer and I stepped out of the van. I was wearing a black chiffon shirt, which was one of the prettier items of clothing I'd packed, a tight black pair of jeans and a plain black pair of flat pumps. I mostly only ever wore black, it was generally a fairly easy colour to coordinate with my limited vision, and thus a good way of avoiding mistakenly buying and wearing something that was neon yellow, for example. And after all, black was meant to be one of the most flattering of colours. Sometimes, when I felt particularly brave, I would venture out into the world of colour too, but only after asking a shop assistant three main questions: Does it look good? Does the colour suit me? And, finally, how would you describe the colour of this? Sometimes the shop assistant would seem baffled, but sometimes not at all. I would then try to suss out whether the assistant was being honest or simply trying their best to sell me the item in question, and I would stare at myself in the shop mirror for ages, trying to visualise what the colour might look like. Sometimes I'd spend a long time locked in a fitting room with my eyes closed, trying to make these visualisations. But usually I wore black, and my everyday decisions of what to wear were based on the feel of the fabric. Who needed colour when you had texture?

We walked towards *The Shack* and as we got near the door I exchanged a few nervous smiles with some people who were lingering outside. They all smiled back, and I felt an overblown sense of relief. *See Silvia, there's nothing to be scared of,* I told myself, *you worry far too much.*

Inside, the place was dark and full of people. It was really just one room, with a bar at one end, and the stage at the opposite end. A dim light illuminated the stage and the wooden panelled wall behind it. I looked around – even in the darkness I could tell the whole place was made of this raw unvarnished wood. I could even smell it, somewhere between the mixture of all the other smells that filled the room: sweat, perfume, beer, bodies and cigarettes. Some people were dancing to a DJ's music, and some were chatting. The music was loud, people had to shout to each other to be heard.

Jack led me to the bar and got us both more beer, then he turned and nodded towards the stage. He nudged me to urge me forward, and as we walked towards the stage he put his hand on the small of my back and guided me forward until we were close to it. In my tipsy state his hand on my body gave me thoughts I tried hard to dismiss. I took three long gulps of beer. We didn't talk, just watched, as the next band were set up on stage. I felt a hint of awkwardness and I wondered if he felt it at all too. At one point he turned round and smiled down at me, placed his hand on my shoulder and said, 'You okay?' I nodded. The band appeared. A pretty blonde fronted it, and they played a mixture of garage rock and country. I looked at Jack from the corner of my eye and saw that he was staring up at them, smiling, and nodding his head to the music. I looked around me and people were beginning to dance. Before long I found my body swaying to the music too.

There was an uproar of shouting and clapping after the band finished their first song. The girl introduced them in a deep southern accent, beaming at the crowd and saying thank you to everyone who'd made it to the gig. The crowd cheered some more and then the band went straight into their next song. It was so incredibly upbeat that in a second the whole room was moving with bodies dancing. Suddenly Jack took my hand and we too were dancing, smiling like two happy-go-lucky youths, and it just didn't feel strange at all. The beer had made my inhibitions disappear and the music led me. I felt a happiness I couldn't remember having experienced for many years. I felt completely carefree and it felt wonderful. And I was sweaty, very sweaty. Strands of wet hair stuck to my face as my whole body shook to the music. I didn't care; I was dancing. I was smiling.

Later that night, when the music had mellowed and quietened, we sat around talking. The alcohol had made us lose the self-consciousness and the words were flowing freely, passionately. I was letting suppressed thoughts out for the first time, vocalising things that I had kept inside and hidden away from even myself.

So this was how it felt to share one's mind.

I suddenly realised that Jack was actually very beautiful. I hadn't noticed it before. No, that's a lie, a total lie. Of course I had noticed, I'd just never wanted to find him attractive. And why had I allowed myself to truly notice and admit it now? Well, I was drunk. Drunk and happy.

'You know,' I said, 'it's good to talk.'

'And dance.'

'Yeah, it's definitely good to dance.'

Before I knew it, we were kissing.

*

We may have had sex in an uncomfortable van in a parking lot in a sudden fit of lust, but it was beautiful. Afterwards, when we lay huddled together, his body against mine, I understood that I had never yet had this kind of sex. I had never been touched like that by a man. His touch seemed completely untainted by arrogance, hesitation or self-protection. Jack didn't seem to restrain himself in any way. After sex I usually avoided 'cuddling' – even the mere word made me feel nauseous. It usually felt insincere, self-conscious… obligatory. This seemed the complete opposite. It felt natural. There was no shame in Jack's affection.

As I lay there awake, smiling to myself, I realised something else. It wasn't just him that had made this experience unique. It was me. This was the first time I'd ever in my life properly let go with a man. It was usually me who restrained myself, but this time I didn't need to because Jack already knew most of my secrets. I had little left to hide. I don't think I'll ever forget how I felt that night, lying in the back of that van, his body around mine.

The next morning was surreal and beautiful. All the cars had gone and *The Shack* was now closed and boarded up, looking as though it had been abandoned many years ago. Around us there were no signs of the buzzing human life that had been there only a few hours ago. Lenticular clouds hung over the jagged sandy lumps on the eastern horizon, and the sun was only just rising – slowly waking and peering out. It had come to greet only me, for in this open dusty space there was not another soul in sight. The long dark shadows cast by the hills and mountains slowly receded, and light poured into the valley.

I had woken before Jack. I put some clothes on and climbed out of the van as quietly as I could so as not to wake him. My head rudely reminded me that last night's alcohol consumption had been a little excessive. My feet hit the ground and I breathed in the air. It smelled like freedom.

I wasn't deluding myself. It's not as though I wasn't aware of the fact that at any point this could all end and something far worse than what I'd ran away from would become my reality. All this I knew and feared. But for a moment, as I stood there looking out at the landscape and the sky, fear vanished, and all I had was my present reality. And presently I was free.

I paced forward a few steps into the sunshine and sat down in the dirt with my back to the van. The air was crisp but not cold. I spotted a bald eagle soaring high up. This was a bird I could recognise and remember way back from my early childhood. Unmistakable. Every now and then a gentle breeze tickled my skin. Silence reigned. All was still. Even the voices in my head seemed to be sleeping.

I sat there for a while trying hard to hold onto this meditative state, until the sun had fully risen over the horizon, spreading its carpet of light across the valley floor, and I heard Jack shuffling around in the van. I didn't turn around at first, pretending I hadn't heard a thing. So what now? I thought to myself. Would there be any awkwardness? I heard him get out of the van and then I heard his footsteps coming towards me. I should probably turn around now, I thought.

'Morning,' he said, rubbing his eyes, 'you're up early.'

'Hey,' I said, trying to sound as casual as possible.

He reached me, sat down and put his arm around me. We sat in silence for a few moments looking out at the landscape. For a while my body remained stiff. I was reluctant to show affection back, in case I'd misunderstood the situation. But what was there to misunderstand? For the first time there was nothing complicated going on, so, finally, I leaned into his hold, to which he responded by holding me a little more tightly. We sat like that for a while longer, saying nothing. I would have gladly sat like it for hours.

'We should probably get out of this place and get some breakfast,' he said.

For a split second I'd totally forgotten we were on the run, I had been lost in a blissful state of oblivion.

We weren't too far from hidden places. As we drove further along, mile after mile, we reached a stretch with thick pine forest on both sides. We turned off onto a small path and once we were far enough from the road Jack stopped and switched off the engine.

I wondered what it was like for him. I knew I was crippled with fear every time I remembered I was hiding, but I wondered if he felt any of that same fear at all. He never showed it. My fear came through personal experience. I feared that at any moment the same people, organisation, whoever killed my parents could show up and kill me, at any moment. Kill *us*. But perhaps he knew better than me how big or small any threat was, and how likely it was that such a thing could happen. He'd studied cases like this, hadn't he? Though, in reality, surely neither of us could really know anything for certain.

Jack had packed a lot of things. He had come well prepared. There were boxes full of cans, bags of pasta, oatmeal, garlic, jars of tomato sauce, apples, sultanas, nuts, crackers, cocoa powder, spices. That morning we had oatmeal and banana for breakfast. But I found it hard to eat. Ever since we'd left the vicinity of *The Shack* my mind had slowly sunk back into that dark place. A carousel of thoughts had taken over me.

'What's up?' he said.

I shook my head.

'Nothing,' I muttered.

There was a few seconds pause in which we both knew I was lying.

'What if they're here?' I whispered.

His shock brought me both relief and embarrassment.

'Are you serious?'

'Well they could be,' I said, suddenly feeling defensive.

'Of course they *could* be. "They" could be anywhere. Or they could be nowhere. Or there may not even be a "they". We don't know. We don't have a clue. We don't even know if what we're running away from is real.'

'This was your fucking idea,' I said, without thinking.

'Look,' he said, 'I'm sorry. You're right. Anything is possible. Right now though, we're in a forest eating breakfast and that's all there is.'

I didn't understand how he could be so relaxed.

'How are you finding all this?' I said.

'How do you mean?'

'Well, that epiphany of yours. How is it to have had a realisation like that, to know that apparently all is well and there's nothing to fear. How is it to know all that and yet be involved in what we're doing now?'

'What, eating?' he laughed.

'Oh, *ha ha*, don't go getting all Zen on me, you know what I mean. This whole thing, running away from a potential danger. I'm fucking scared. Aren't you?'

It took him a while to reply.

'Yes,' he said, 'I guess sometimes I am.' He paused. 'But I check myself, and ask what it is I'm actually scared of and why.'

'So you question your fears?'

He shrugged and then nodded, 'of course'.

'I do that too. Sometimes I wonder if I'm just running away from my own imagination. But I've also thought about death a lot. I've had to,' I said.

He looked at me. He reached out his hand and placed it on my arm.

'I don't just mean about my mother,' I said. 'I've thought about death in more ways than one. I kept quiet all that time because I feared that if I didn't keep the secret they'd find me and kill me. That's what I fear most. That someone will come when I least expect it. That's probably paranoia, I know. But because I've lived with this fear for so long I've also had a lot of time to address it. Death is inevitable, and potentially always just around the corner. Sooner or later it'll come. I'm terrified of death, Jack. But I've also had moments where I've wanted to just disappear. Existence is fleeting, no matter who you are. So I guess I just wanted to know why it is I fear death. What about death makes it so scary? Is there a possibility of losing the fear of it? I haven't come up with any definitive answers yet. Obviously. And I don't believe in God. Or heaven. So…'

He was nodding.

'Actually, I've often thought about death and fear in exactly the same way,' he said, 'I guess the fear of death is the fear of the unknown. And the fear of loss maybe, of losing life, but then, what is life anyway? And is life something you have or something you are? And is death really the opposite of life? Or the opposite of birth? Can life have an opposite? Isn't life all there is?'

'But, if I die, I lose my life.'

'You lose your life… it's a funny phrase, isn't it? Makes it sound like there are two things there: something called "you", and something called "your life".'

I thought about what he said for a few seconds.

'So…?' I said. 'That's just playing with words, it doesn't mean anything. The "I" and "my life" are the same thing.'

'I get what you're saying, but I guess I'm just wondering what the *I* is anyway.'

He turned himself towards me.

'Where are you?' he said.

'What do you mean?'

'It's not a trick question. Where are you?'

'Here,' I said, pointing to myself.

'What… here?' he said, pointing from my head to my feet.

'Yeah,' I said shrugging, 'that's me.'

'So your body? You are your body?'

'Well yes, I guess. But obviously not only my body. My brain as well… I mean my mind.'

'Do you mean your thoughts?'

'I guess so.'

'But if you are your thoughts, then what is the thing that knows you're thinking?'

I contemplated this question for a little while.

'Awareness, I guess.'

'Yes,' he said, and after a long pause he added, 'but now what is this thing called awareness?'

'Death can't possibly be the end,' I circled back to the topic at hand after a long pause, 'because why would any of this have happened – my life, this life, Silvia – if after death that was just the end of it. It wouldn't make sense.'

'Maybe death *is* the end of Silvia, the end of Jack,' he said, 'but maybe it's not *the* end, because maybe there's more here than just a Silvia and a Jack… more going on here than just two stories and two identities with a beginning and an end. Maybe you're more than just a Silvia.'

We packed up the van and started the day's drive, while I carried on thinking.

'So sometimes you get totally caught up in the story of Jack, in your story,' I said, 'and other times you see that Jack is just a story… but is it almost like you live in two realities then?'

He was silent for a long while.

'I'm not sure…I don't think so.'

'Why? Because you see only one of them as reality and the other as an illusion?'

'No,' he laughed, 'it's just, I don't even know what reality is.'

After our late start, our stops on the road were limited and short that day. My mind was full of thought throughout the journey, and by the time we reached a suitable place to park up for the night, I was exhausted. I climbed into the back of the van by myself, whilst he worked on his laptop at the front.

Does Silvia experience life, or does life experience Silvia? This was the question that floated round in my head as I drifted off to sleep that night.

A Thousand Needles

I looked at him and didn't say a word but just laughed and shook my head. He was smiling back at me.

'Well,' he said, 'shall we?'

I nodded, bit my lip and laughed again. But there was not even an ounce of doubt in me. I was actually looking forward to it. I threw off my sneakers, socks, shorts and sweater. A sudden biting gust of wind made me gasp. He laughed.

'Okay,' he said.

He turned around and ran towards the lake's shore. I followed him, hugging myself from the cold, and hopping to avoid sharp stones. He was already knee deep in the water and had turned to await me.

'And?' I said.

'And it's cold!' he said.

The water was far, far colder than the air. My toes felt numb as soon as they touched it. But I waded in further. Foot deep… ankle deep… calf deep… knee deep, all the while clutching my hands at my chest and repeating the word *fuck!* He turned back around to walk further in. And when he was hip deep he let out a little yelp and dove in, submerging his whole body. He was under for a few seconds and then emerged, shaking the water off his hair and looking at me with the biggest grin I had yet seen on his face. It was ridiculous.

'It gets much warmer after a while,' he said.

I couldn't say anything. I was concentrating too hard. And after a while I simply decided to run in further as fast as I could, still shouting *fuck fuck fuck*, and I finally threw myself down like a sack of potatoes and yelled at the top of my voice. *Shit fuck shit, oh my god, fuck.* He was laughing uncontrollably. *Oh my god.* I was gasping. We were both gasping, stunned by the cold. And then I too couldn't stop laughing, like a maniac. With our heads bobbing above the surface our laughter was interspersed with the chattering of teeth.

'Go under,' he said, 'and open your eyes. You won't regret it.'

Without giving myself time to think or question it, I gulped, held my breath and dove under. It felt like glass shattering over my head, like a thousand needless piercing my skin. I opened my eyes. It was a little murky, but I could see rays of light streaming in and hitting rocks and algae. I was back up in a split second, too cold to stay under for any longer.

'Beautiful, isn't it?' he said.

'Yup.'

It was beautiful, though I imagined that what he could see looked far more beautiful. The colours must have been incredible. I almost felt a pang of jealousy, but that subsided immediately. The cold didn't give me a chance to think stupid thoughts. I quickly took a few strokes back to the shallows. My feet felt totally numb as they slid around on the slimy rocks below. My muscles were stiff. But I was grinning like an insane person. I felt like a child. We were screaming, gasping, laughing and splashing. We were children.

I jumped up, tilted my head back, looked up at the sky and roared, as a wave of euphoria soared through my body.

Not even a whole two minutes after entering the water, I started striding back out, still laughing, still elated, teeth chattering. I looked down at the goose bumps on my body. I had the impression that my limbs were about to fall off, and I couldn't feel my feet as I walked.

But slowly, as I jumped and shook about on the shore, feeling started seeping back into my skin.

With my shaking hands I picked up my sweater and attempted to dry my body off with it. But I didn't have the patience, and so instead I started layering the clothes back onto my damp body. My frozen fingers fiddled and struggled so much with the buttons on my sweater that in the end I gave up on them.

Jack was still in the water, properly swimming now, doing the front crawl. I was doing star jumps and stamping my feet. I was shivering. And yet, somehow, the exhilaration didn't leave me. I danced about on the shore like an idiot, trying to soak up the last rays of the evening sun. When Jack finally came out about five minutes later, he found me curled up, kneeling on the ground, head down, hugging myself and rocking back and forth.

'You need to get out of those damp clothes,' he said.

'My boobs...' I said, still rocking back and forth, 'feels... like... they've fallen off.'

We went back to the van, dried off with a towel and changed into dry clothes. Dusk was approaching. We got the stove out, and cursed ourselves for not having prepared the equipment earlier as we struggled to put the gear together and open packets and tins with our numb hands.

We sat opposite each other with the stove between us as we waited for the spaghetti to cook, taking turns to heat our hands above the steam every now and then. With the blood rushing back, my scar seemed to glow more obviously than ever. The shivering subsided and slowly a glowing warmth came over me. Finally I felt better able to hold a conversation.

'So,' he said, 'how do you feel after your first wild cold water swim?'

I thought for a few seconds, grinning into the air.

'Alive,' I said, 'very very fucking alive.'

*

That night, as we lay wrapped around each other in the back of the van, I felt so close to him. I wondered if now was a good time to tell him, because my mind wouldn't rest until I did.

*

Silvia: 2:30am, Sunday 1 July 2007

Oh wow. I'm buzzing. This night has definitely been a turning point. We just had a house party and I am one hundred per cent drunk. And high. That's right. Silvia did alcohol and drugs for the first time tonight! I danced so much and hung out with so many cool people and no one thought I was weird! It was amazing!

Oh god, but I'm so drunk...

Donny: 2:45am, Sunday 1 July 2007

Mom and Dad are away this weekend and so, of course, I organised a party. It was definitely better than Jared Hartley's party two weeks ago, and he's the high school jock, so I'm feeling pretty proud of myself. I'm also feeling pretty drunk.

Most people have gone home, but some are sleeping downstairs in the lounge, some in mine and Silvia's rooms. We've managed to keep mom and dad's room out of bounds. Silvia's been pretty cool about the whole party thing, I thought she'd protest but she didn't. I think she actually had fun.

I say goodnight to the boys downstairs. They're all shitfaced and already half asleep. Josh says hey man, gnarly party, and immediately starts snoring. I climb up the stairs with a bottle of beer. Mine and Silvia's rooms are full and there's even some kid sleeping in the hallway. The place is totally trashed, but we've got the whole of tomorrow to clear up. I should be taking photos of the state of the house now as proof of how rad the party was. I go to Mom and Dad's room and Silvia's already lying on the bed, watching TV and... smoking a joint! No way! Where'd she get that from?

The room is dark except for the light from the TV. I climb onto the bed, get comfortable and Silvia hands me the joint. I grin. She's both drunk and high and she's laughing. She looks pretty hot in the dark. Who am I kidding. She is hot.

I barely get to smoke any of the joint. We're kissing pretty much immediately. Silvia's clearly never kissed anyone before but she's actually not so bad at it. I wonder if the same goes for the sex.

Despite being shitfaced drunk I manage to get it up. Today is a success day and I feel pretty good about myself. The sex is all right, she's not an expert but then neither am I — I've only ever slept with two other girls before, and only the one time with each… and that was over a year ago…

Donny: Thursday 6 August 2009

I'm standing in the queue at Carla's Café ready to order, when Silvia walks through the entrance. There's no way of avoiding her, she'll look up and see me any second now.

She's seen me. Oh my god, Donny, *she says.* We haven't seen each other for almost a year. I think we were both hoping we'd never see each other again. I've pretty much avoided every reunion Mom and Dad have had with her since she moved out.

The stuff we did behind Mom and Dad's back was pretty weird, but I think it's high time she got over it. We were never actual brother and sister so it's not as creepy as she made it out to be.

How are you? *I tell her I'm okay, and soon we're sitting at the same table and having coffee together. She tells me about her art and I tell her about how I'm training to be a police officer. I'm surprised at how good her English has become. I ask her if I can see any of her art and she tells me she doesn't have any of her work on her to show me now, but she doesn't live too far from here if I want to come see. I say okay.*

Her apartment is amazing. It's full of flowers and books. I wonder what books she's been reading, how smart she is and if I should be worried. She tells me she does loads of abstract stuff and still life. Flower paintings are currently her thing, she says. She's obsessed. There are thousands of different flowers everywhere. Her art is pretty good. All her paintings and drawings are in black and white and I suddenly remember that of course she can't see colour.

I ask her if she's ever painted nudes before, she says no, but she smirks when she says it. I ask her if she wants to. She shrugs. I ask her if she wants to try now and she says Donny, shut up! *but she's definitely still smirking.*

Soon enough I'm naked and she is actually drawing me. This is great, I'm actually going to do it with Silvia again, I never saw this coming!

It gets cold when you're naked and have to sit still. I ask her if she's finished. She says almost *and I say* hurry up. *When she is finished though, she has a huge smile on her face.* Donny, *she says,* I fucking love drawing nudes! Thank you! *She tells me that from now on she only wants to ever draw naked bodies.* It's like flowers but way, way better, *she says. She's found herself a new obsession.*

We're both laughing. The drawing is pretty good. But I'm still naked and now I'm horny. I press myself against her from behind and start kissing her neck. She jumps away. Donny! *She says, and she looks horrified.* What? *I say.* No, *she says,* no, no, no. *And she's shaking her head.* What the fuck Silvia? I've just sat naked for you for almost an hour in the cold. You fucking owe me! *She looks even more horrified now and I realise what I just said probably sounded pretty bad, but I think to myself we grew up together, I'm allowed to talk to her like that. She's practically my sister!*

We get into a fight. We're shouting at each other and swear words are flying around while I'm dressing myself. I'm so fucking angry. I haven't been this angry in ages. You fucking slut, *I say,* you're just a cheap fucking whore, with dumbass parents who got themselves killed because they were loud mouth hippies. Fuck you and fuck them!

Oh fuck. Oh shit.

She's gone silent. What did you say? *she says. First quietly and then louder.* What did you say? What the fuck did you just say? *I sigh. What have I done? I've really gone and said it, haven't I? I've really just gone and done it. And I repeat myself in a more diplomatic way.*

She refuses to let me leave. She's gone psycho and she's actually holding a knife and crying and I can't tell whether she's threatening me with the knife or threatening to hurt herself. But she says she wants every last detail. She wants to know what I know.

I tell her the basics. She asks me loads of questions. I knew it. I knew it, *she keeps repeating.*

She asks me about the money she gets each month from Mom and Dad. Where does it come from? *she asks.* How am I supposed to know?! I don't fucking know, *I say, because I really don't. She's yelling now and I'm hoping to fuck no one else can hear her.* Why didn't they kill me? Why didn't they fucking kill me?! *I tell her I have no idea. She doesn't believe me.* Why didn't they just pull the trigger? It would have been so easy. So much easier than all this, *she says, gesturing at the apartment. It had never even occurred to me that she might have been there when her parents were killed. This is more fucked up than I ever knew. I just know who her parents were and why they were gotten rid of. I overheard Mom and Dad talking about it once. Now I wish I never had.*

I can't believe I let all this slip after all those years. I can't fucking believe it. How am I going to cover my back? I need to tell her it's dangerous. I need to scare her into silence. I tell her she can't ever tell anyone any of this. I tell her that if anyone finds out that'll be the end of her. I don't mince my words. And before I leave I tell her not to contact me ever again.

Silvia: Thursday 6 August 2009

I lie on the kitchen floor amongst the debris. Broken glass, plates, cups… I stare up at the fuzz of ceiling and I imagine cockroaches crawling over me. I am death. My right hand pulsates as warm blood oozes out onto the floor. I didn't want to hurt myself. Silly Silvia. I should have been more careful in my rage. But now that I lie here with the dark flooding the room, I imagine all my blood slowly seeping out of me overnight, and the thought doesn't seem so bad. It seduces me.

Today I have learned three very different things. The truth about why my parents died. What I love to draw most. And that I must now learn to draw with my left hand. Perhaps I won't wake tomorrow. I laugh my way to oblivion.

Claustrophobia

The dreams are more regular now. Fuelled by the fears that come with this journey. Night after night I see the same scene. My mother being killed before me. I hear the two gunshots so vividly, exactly as they sounded the night it happened. They were so real, so audible in my dream, as if no amount of time could fade out the memory. They were just as real now as they had been those seventeen years ago. Bang. The first shot. My mother to my right, our bodies brush against each other as we sit up in alarm. Footsteps to the door, lights on, two men, bang, the second shot. I feel the bed jolt as her body falls back and her head hits the pillow. I look at her, blood seeping out of her chest. The gun is pointing at me. Will he shoot? This is the moment I wake up, bolt upright. I'm breathing heavily and quickly. It's dark all around. I'm so scared. Jack has reached over to me and is holding me. I'm crying. He's telling me it's okay. He's holding me close and he's telling me it's okay.

Everything's okay. It was all just a dream.

*

It was still dark outside when Jack woke me, but we had a long day's drive ahead of us and we needed to get going. Our time at the Crater Lake National Park had been incredible. I couldn't fathom how it was possible that I was finally letting myself go like that with someone… with a man. We drove for around fourteen hours that day, with barely any stops. Jack didn't talk much, it seemed as though he had some things on his mind, secrets of his own.

Jack had been, understandably, pretty annoyed that I hadn't told him about Donny from the start. He said it changed a lot, a fucking great deal in fact.

My memories of what I did with Donny were filled with confusion, disgust, shame and regret. It hadn't been easy to talk about.

Yes, we drove in silence that day.

A couple of hours before we reached the border, Jack took a turn off the highway, followed a few roads and we came to a track in the middle of some secluded fields surrounded by forests.

'Right,' he said, as he stopped the van, 'we need to hide you.'

'Hide me?'

He climbed out of the van and went to the back. I followed. He opened the boot, told me to wait a minute and he climbed into the back and started rummaging through boxes and arranging things differently. *Hide me?* After about ten minutes of fiddling around in the back he turned round and looked at me.

'I think this will be fairly easy,' he said, 'because you're tiny.'

He then proceeded to reveal a secret compartment in the floor of the van and showed me how to climb into it. What the fuck? Instead of feeling fear it seemed my body skipped that part and went straight to a strange paralysis. My arms felt limp as he reached to help me up into the van. I was tingling all over.

He talked me through the instructions: when to climb in, how to close it, something about breathing, something about staying calm. As I tried the compartment out for size, I felt like I was squeezing into a coffin. He kept asking me if I was okay. I just kept nodding.

'Just remember,' he said before shutting the boot, 'once we cross the border you're safe.'

Later, when I was surrounded by total blackness, tucked away in that tiny suffocating compartment that smelled of warm plastic, everything turned into a hazy blur. I wasn't quite unconscious but, I don't remember much. I lost track of time completely. I have no idea how long any of it took. All I knew was that there was no way I was ever doing this again. There was no way Jack would be taking me to Alaska.

Oak

The dog climbed into our van without hesitation. She was at my feet, lying there suddenly, as though this was the most normal of things. She was panting and staring into the air with a stupid happy look on her face. I reached for a bottle of water and poured some into an empty peanut can. She looked up at me with her big grateful eyes and lapped up all the water in a few seconds. She couldn't have been any older than one, if even that.

We'd found her the day after the crossing. I was feeling so much better that day – the worst was already behind me. No one knew I was here, and it was like Jack had said, I was safer now. We could slow down. We hovered around the outskirts of Vancouver whilst Jack did some work on my case. He was also trying to plan where we'd go next, now that I'd messed up his plan by declaring that I refused to go to Alaska. I was not getting into that coffin of a compartment again. Yesterday's tensions about my decision, as well as about Donny, had been momentary. Jack had a way of not harbouring grudges and I admired him for it. It wasn't at all that he was a pushover, he fought his case, but in the end he realised I was totally decided. Then he told me he had every intention of going to Alaska himself at some point, with or without me. He soon changed the subject though, and any ounce of negativity between us disappeared – for now we were just too relaxed for any of that.

That night we'd parked up in a big clearing surrounded by forest. It was used as a parking lot but it was empty when we got there. I heard just one car come and go in the early morning, while it was still dark outside. Jack had sensed my fear, wrapped his arms around me and pressed his body against mine, without saying a word. But the car soon left, as suddenly as it had arrived.

Now that it was morning I was preparing some coffee while Jack was inside the van with the door open, looking at a map. Over the hiss of the stove I heard a whimper coming from somewhere behind me. I wasn't sure if I hadn't just imagined it but I got up out of curiosity. I walked past a section of bushes. In front of a trail that led into the forest stood a long low wooden gate, and there, in front of that gate, a small dog was standing and sniffing the earth. Her ribs protruded out of her tiny frail body and her eyes gazed longingly at me.

'Hey doggy,' I said, 'where's your owner?'

From what I could see, she was a girl. I approached her slowly, but I quickly realised that she didn't have a tag. My heart sunk as it dawned on me that the car that had come early that morning had probably abandoned her. I went back to the van. As I finished making the coffee I tried not to look at the poor mutt too much because I knew the eye contact could give her hope. When I was a kid I'd come across tons of strays and I knew that, unless you were going to take the dog home with you, you shouldn't show it any affection. It was unfair on the dog to give it such false hope.

But, from the corner of my eye, I could see that she was still there. Her head hung low, her tail was stuck between her hind legs. She was a pitiful sight. After finishing my coffee I went to pour out the remains a few metres away from the van. The sound of her paws on the gravel told me she had followed me. Though it broke my heart I tried to shoo her away, but she carried on traipsing behind. Perhaps she could sense that every time I waved my arm to try to get her to go away, it was twitching to reach out and touch her fur and stroke her little body.

Jack was even worse at attempting to ignore her. He'd actually ended up getting out of the van and was now stroking her. He'd clearly not had as much experience with stray dogs as I'd had in my life.

And now she had followed us back to the van. What could we do? She was inside. It was definitely her choice more than ours. We hadn't discussed it but neither of us protested either. An unspoken agreement.

'What should we call her?' I asked.

Jack laughed.

'Sandy?' he said.

'No, that's shit!' I said bluntly.

He looked around him for inspiration. From the dashboard he picked up the knife we used to cut food with. He read the small words at the bottom of the wooden handle.

'Made in Philippines,' he said.

I laughed.

'Philip!' I said.

'She's a female for god's sake!' he laughed.

'Philippa then!'

We thought about it.

'Nah,' we said simultaneously.

'Nice names,' he said, 'but not for a dog.'

'Oak!' I exclaimed suddenly, pointing at the handle of the knife. 'Oak! Oak's a good name!'

'Yes,' he looked at me and smiled, 'I love it! Oak!'

'Hey Oak,' we said to her, 'hey Oaky.'

Oak looked up at us, tilted her head and started wagging her tale madly. Jack and I looked at each other and burst out laughing. And so it stuck, Oak, our new companion. I didn't know then just how important a part of my life she would become.

*

That night as we lay in the dark of the van, Jack took my right hand, brought it to his lips and kissed my scar.

'Thank you,' he whispered. 'Thank you for sharing.'

He didn't say anything else. He didn't have to.

Isabelle

'Thank you Isabelle,' he said, with a smile on his face.

The girl at the till looked startled, but she quickly realised what he'd done, and she blinked down at her name badge and blushed.

'Oh,' she said, with a slight giggle, 'that's quite all right, have a great day!'

As we walked out of the shop towards the van Jack was still smiling, in his own world, as though I wasn't there. We got into the van, he placed the shopping bags behind us and got comfortable in his seat. All the while I was staring at him. He finally noticed.

'What?' he said.

'What was all that about?'

'What was all what about?'

'The girl,' I said, ' "Oh thank you Isabelle",' I said, mimicking him.

I was laughing, trying my best to seem cool and blasé, but it was too late, my jealousy was obvious. Isabelle wasn't particularly remarkable or stunning and so far he hadn't looked at anyone else's name badge to tell them a personal thank you. Why her?

'Oh, Isabelle?'

'Yes, Isabelle,' I said, 'do you know her?'

'No. But I used to know an Isabelle. She was great,' he said smiling.

My blood suddenly boiled. I think my face went red. *It's okay Silvia, ex-girlfriends don't mean a thing,* I told myself. He turned around to me and let out a soft sigh before facing the road and pulling out of the lot.

'I'll tell you all about that at the next stop,' he said.

'Where are we going?'

'You'll see,' he said.

As we drove it dawned on me just how little I still knew about Jack.

Sproat Lake

We were heading to Vancouver Island, another place I knew nothing about, but that Jack seemed to know a lot about already. After purchasing tickets we drove onto the ferry and in less than two hours we reached the island. Another one and a half hour drive and we reached a big lake, where Jack stopped the van.

During that whole journey, since Jack had thanked Isabelle in the store over four hours ago, we'd barely spoken to each other. Now at the lake with its forested shores, Jack switched off the engine, and we took some food and a rug out of the van. We walked over to a wooden picnic table where we set all our stuff down. We sat down, opposite each other, each a bench to ourselves. Oak curled herself up at my feet. Jack perched himself at the end of his bench, hanging his legs off the side, so he was side on to me and facing the lake.

'Sproat Lake,' he said without looking at me, 'beautiful, isn't it? Even prettier than the pictures.'

I hadn't seen any pictures, I knew nothing, but I nodded. So was this the next stop he'd been talking about? The place he was going to tell me about this mysterious Isabelle? My heart sunk. I didn't really want to know anymore.

*

Jack's little sister had been twenty-two years old when she was diagnosed with malignant melanoma. Terminal. Six weeks later she died. Now I understood why, despite the fact he said he loved it, Jack avoided the sun the way he did.

Jack had never been particularly close to either of his parents – least of all his father. Jack's dad had always wanted him to study corporate law, and many tensions and confrontations had arisen between the two due to the differences in their ideological beliefs. But Jack had always been close to his sister, Isabelle. Though there were only five years between the two, she would always be the little baby sister, and he the overly protective big brother. Isabelle was small and slender, and had a long mane of golden red locks, huge blue eyes, pale skin and freckled nose: a good giveaway of the family's Irish roots. But she loved the sun. Since as far back as Jack could remember, Isabelle would always be outside as soon as the sun was out. Everybody loves the sunshine, but Isabelle was addicted.

And she was beautiful, sun-kissed and glowing. According to Jack, she was that rare mix – attractive, intelligent and kind.

'You know,' said Jack half laughing, 'one of those girls who gets stopped, interviewed and photographed by a style magazine, and they ask her where she got her "cute little sweater" from and she's all like, "oh my goodness, thank you! Oh, this thing? I got it from a thrift store…" and all this whilst she's in a bit of a hurry because she's on her way to volunteer at the women's refuge on a weekday evening, or the animal shelter on the weekend.' Jack rolled his eyes and smiled sadly. 'Isabelle was that girl,' he continued. 'And man, she was a heartbreaker. It sure made it hard to be her brother; I had to deal with loads of jerks. She always looked immaculate. I guess that was the main difference between me and her. I just didn't care!'

'Oh, but guys that don't give a shit… they have their charm.' I smirked at him.

'Ha! Yes, the same goes for girls…'

I wondered if I was the kind of girl that generally gave a shit or didn't give a shit. I wondered which one Jack thought I was.

The day I bumped into Jack in Balboa Park he had been thinking about Isabelle a lot. Perhaps that's the reason he felt like opening up to a stranger about his thoughts on life and death. Isabelle's death was a reminder of what he'd glimpsed on that beach. A reminder of the utterly beautiful ridiculousness of existence.

The day Jack found out about Isabelle's cancer it didn't even cross his mind that his sister was going to die. He was sure she was going to be okay as soon as the doctors sorted her out. Isabelle thought the same. She talked a lot about visiting him in San Diego again at some point soon, after graduating. They wanted to do a road trip, all the way from San Diego to Alaska.

Jack went on to tell me about how Isabelle had affected his relationship with Adam. Back during their university days, when Adam and Jack had only recently met, they were involved in a range of protests, a few of which had turned violent. On one occasion Jack had been arrested for throwing a brick in the direction of a group of police officers – except Jack hadn't done it, they must have confused him with someone else. But the officers refused to listen and he was taken to jail. Adam bailed him out and from that day the friendship was sealed, they were inseparable.

It just so happened that over the years, in an attempt to battle his anxiety and depression, Adam had developed a strong interest in Eastern philosophy. In his spare time, when he wasn't working himself up talking or thinking about the state of the world, and the greed-driven economic and political structures that ran it, Adam was very much a spiritual seeker. He had a whole library of books to prove it. Books on Zen, Taoism, Advaita, transcendental meditation, self-realisation, and the like. And Adam could sit for hours attempting to meditate his way to enlightenment. But when Adam found out about Jack's epiphany, instead of feeling happy for his friend, Adam was jealous. He was jealous that Jack, who'd never even dabbled in spirituality, never meditated, never even come across the term *enlightenment* in its spiritual context, was graced with the random luck of such a powerful awakening, whilst Adam was still getting his panic attacks.

Their friendship started to crumble. Jack told me that it was strange to suddenly realise that the friendship had turned out to be mainly based on shared radical political views. Jack was finding himself increasingly ready to phase Adam's growing negativity out of his life.

But things changed in the last weeks of Isabelle's life, when she was fighting to live. Adam had known Isabelle fairly well, and the news of her cancer had devastated him. He'd liked her from the start, but had never acted on it. The distance was too great to try to start something, let alone the difficulties of being in a relationship with your best friend's little sister. With Isabelle's death, Adam remembered how much he actually cared for Jack. Her death rekindled their friendship in a completely new way.

There were just too many ties between the two to keep them separated. Too much history – shared experiences that only they knew about. And it was Isabelle, beautiful wonderful Isabelle, who somehow managed to reconfigure everything. The tragedy of her death deepened Jack and Adam's friendship. It was thanks to her that the friendship endured.

'Isn't it strange how things happen like that sometimes? Life is a continual chain of loss and gain. The only constant is change.'

I smiled, but the waxing and waning of friendships was not something I knew much about.

'Meditation is a funny thing,' Jack said after a pause. 'People think that if they meditate they'll reach nirvana. They think nirvana is something you can attain if you put in the hours and the dedication. Being a seeker is like a whole identity, you know. It's like a full time job. You become more interested in seeking than in finding. I'm not saying meditation is bad. In terms of psychological health benefits, it must be great.'

'So what, you can't attain nirvana?'

'Everything already is nirvana. We can't see it because we're looking for it.'

I laughed. 'Like the fish swimming in the sea looking for water?'

'Yes,' he smiled, 'just like that goddamned fish.'

'But then, not everyone's looking for nirvana.'

'Aren't they? New car, new lover, new house, sex, drugs, rock 'n' roll... isn't it all just our attempt at reaching fulfilment?'

I shrugged. 'So this is nirvana?'

'Absolutely,' he said.

I laughed and so did he.

And after a pause he added, 'but it can also be hell, for those who can't see it.'

I could still sense how much he'd loved his sister. It was good to hear someone else's story for a change, instead of just being trapped in my own one. I thought about how, as an adult, I'd never really had to show sympathy to anyone. I wondered if that showed. Maybe I wasn't good in these sorts of situations. I wanted to reach out to him, but I wasn't sure exactly how, I wanted to tell him I was glad he'd told me all this. I felt an urge to somehow reach out in the same way he'd reached out to me. I suddenly saw Jack as a fragile human being, and I had never thought he was.

*

The water in the lake was so clean and clear that you could see down to the bottom even when you swam into the depths. It smelled so intensely fresh it was like breathing for the first time. It was so much warmer than my last swim, and I must have stayed in there for almost half an hour, taking in the views of the beaches and Douglas Fir forests that lined it. Shades and contrast appeared stronger than usual in the light of this crisp summer day. Oak, though she occasionally barked after us, waited patiently at the shore, showing no interest whatsoever in joining us in the water. As I floated on the lake's surface, lying still, looking up at the sky with my ears submerged in the lake's silence, I contemplated the vastness of the universe. Here I was looking up at an infinite sky. I was but a tiny speck floating on a miniscule puddle, floating on a spherical object floating in space. With perspective like that what was there to ever worry about?

Light at Cox Bay

Jack pointed up the beach to the silhouette of the Lennard Island lighthouse in the distance.

'There's something about lighthouses,' he said. 'As a kid it was my dream to one day live in one.'

I nodded. We were sitting on a beach at Cox Bay, still on Vancouver Island. Seagulls screeched and waves crashed as we breathed in the smell of ocean. Oak was curled up in the sand, dozing. Jack had just finished drying off, clothing himself and gulping down some tea after a cold swim. I had watched him as he bodysurfed on the waves. It looked incredible when he did that. How *did* he do it? He made it look so easy. We were eating our evening meal of peanut butter sandwiches, and soaking up the last warming rays of sun.

'I guess there's something very romantic about the idea, isn't there?' I said.

'Totally. It's so easy to imagine a secluded life, surrounded by the force of the ocean, far away from the rush, turmoil and monotony of city living. You know, a poetic life,' he laughed.

He was right. I found myself fantasising about living a secret life with him, tucked away in a lighthouse, far away from civilisation – a place where no one would ever find us... and we'd live happily ever after... I was completely in the throes of a childish fantasy.

'What are you smiling about?' he asked.

If only he knew. 'Nothing,' I said, 'I'm just imagining how nice our lighthouse would be. Like in Moominland or something,' I laughed.

He laughed with me and nodded.

'Yeah, I guess most of those childhood ideas I had in my head pretty much did belong to fantasy. I don't know how things are now, they've probably changed, but back in the day being a lighthouse keeper meant a low wage, constant work, and yeah the isolation might be nice at first but after a while it might drive you mad, and you'd have had little freedom or money to go on holiday...' he paused for a while, 'but maybe that wouldn't be so bad,' he said, 'I don't know, I guess different people react differently to different situations. Some people like being alone.'

'Do you?' I asked.

He shrugged. We lay there on the sand for a while, both staring up at the open sky above us, both in our own worlds. I thought about Jack and what he'd told me about Isabelle. I felt closer to him after that conversation. And with that closeness I'd begun to feel a growing calmness.

When the air began to cool we gathered up our things and walked aimlessly along the shore. And as we walked he told me that the seas of British Columbia had once teemed with salmon, as though there was a never ending supply, and how in the early nineties the accumulation of human greed and the waste encouraged by commercial fishing had finally taken its toll, bringing the fish close to extinction. He told me all this, with dates and figures, names and places, like my mother would have done had she been here. I felt like I was in a strange and wonderful place, flittering between nostalgia and intense presence. Memories of the sweet parts of my childhood, combined with something – Jack, the road, the landscapes – that didn't belong at all to the past nor the future, but only to a *now* I suddenly cherished so much.

I was overwhelmed with the feeling that this was an incredible interlude in my life. I could have never imagined any of it. Here I was with a man and a dog that a couple of months ago did not exist to me, in a place that I never knew existed either.

When I forgot my fears, about the idea that we were running away, that danger existed, all I was left with was the magic of the world that surrounded me – the landscapes, the light, the sky – and this incredible connection I felt with my two travelling companions. It seemed there were two worlds, the world of fear, and this world of magic. And I wondered which was truer of the two.

As the sun sunk towards Lennard Island, the silhouette of the lighthouse looked like a huge sea creature with a long protruding neck, on top of which was a head with two bright eyes. It was as though he had slowly risen from the sea to watch me. A distant watchful presence. And with this lighthouse-turned-sea-creature, everything else seemed to glow with some strange fantastical quality too. *Like Moominland*, I thought. I let out a short laugh under my breath. But I really did feel like I was in some kind of wonderland.

With my feet pressed into the sand I watched the foaming edge of the surf. It was joyfully playing a game with itself, seeing how far it could reach before it decided to retreat once again. And as the water pulled back, the froth that was left bubbled and fizzed with an intensity I hadn't noticed before. I looked back at my shadow. I waved at it and it waved back. Between the sun and the earth stood a me. A me that was solid enough to cast a shadow. And I looked back at the sun and, in an instant, all there was was light. For a brief moment it felt as though there was not a me looking at light, but just light. Light seeing light.

I was floating in a sea of warm glowing light.

'Look, Silvia, look!'

I snapped back to my senses and quickly turned towards where Jack was pointing. At first I didn't see a thing, and then, out there on the horizon two whales jumped out from beneath the ocean. They danced out there for a few minutes, for our eyes only. They were grey whales, Jack told me. Finally the ocean swallowed them up, and they disappeared back into the vast depths from which they had come.

I will never forget that evening on the beach. It changed me. Fear no longer had such a firm grip. I wondered what the future held, and then I stopped wondering, for it wasn't long before the immediacy and intimacy of my present reality bewildered me once again. The light, the play of contrast on land, sea and sky, the sound of waves, the water breathing in... out... in... out, the taste and smell of salty ocean air, Jack's skin on mine as the weight of our bodies pressed against each other, a soft breeze. This was my world.

*

For the next couple of days we explored more of the island. As we walked through forests of Red Cedar and Douglas Fir and along windswept beaches, and drove slowly along misty roads, I felt strangely unlike myself. The beauty of this island was making me forget myself, lose myself – still on a high from the evening at Cox Bay. If I die, I thought, looking around and breathing the world in, at least I will have seen and experienced all this.

We were walking through the old-growth forest like two kids without a care in the world, marvelling at the ancient moss-covered trees that towered above us. It was a very hot day, but under the canopy of the trees the temperature felt perfect. We were both beaming. Even Oak seemed happier than usual. I couldn't remember a time I'd ever smiled so much. Jack tried to describe some of the colours to me. He told me now that apart from the shots of yellow, red or brown, we were most definitely in the very heart of the Kingdom of Green. God, how I longed to see what he could see!

'Some of these will be almost a thousand years old,' he said as he walked up to a tall Western Red Cedar and patted the trunk with his hand.

I walked up to the tree and looked up.

'I feel tiny,' I said.

Once, long ago, this strong, wide and tall tower had been just a small seed. As if by magic, energy had erupted out of the seed in slow motion. Shooting straight up out of the earth, for no apparent reason other than to simply live and to be. How strange these things we called trees were. And weren't we the same? Once just a tiny cell, we grew and grew, a magic explosion of energy and potential. Except that we didn't have a thousand years to keep growing. But perhaps that didn't matter. Perhaps no amount of time would ever seem enough for us anyway. As I looked up I wondered how the tree experienced this thing called time. Surely, without a self-conscious human mind, for the tree life was timeless, an eternal present. And surely that was enough. I put my hand on its soft stringy bark. I looked at Jack.

'Fucking hippies,' I said.

We both laughed and he grabbed my waist and kissed me. His kisses ran to my neck as we sunk down and sat under the tree. He passed a hand beneath my t-shirt and with the tips of his fingers he stroked the bare skin on my stomach… then my back… until I felt my whole body tingling and I was covered in goose bumps. We undressed each other and sat naked under that tree. He traced the contours of my body with his hands. Slowly. Slowly. *Oh Jack…* They ran down from my neck, circled over my breasts, down over my stomach… closer… closer…

This was my favourite thing: the tips of his fingers running over my skin. Before Jack, no one had ever done this to me, no one had ever touched me like this. Gently. Gently. Light as a feather. We could lie there for what seemed like hours on end, touching each other like this, our eyes closed, encapsulated in the silence of the moment. I'd never known sex could be so… beautiful.

Finally, I lay back on that soft carpet of moss, feeling as though I would melt into the earth. Through half open eyes I watched as above me the silhouette of branches and leaves swayed against a white sky. Rays of light shimmered through them. They danced to the rhythm of a slow breeze that blew high above and that only they could feel. I watched them, hypnotised. Jack towered over me. Those dancing silhouettes and light now surrounded his face and were like an aura glowing around him.

Time stood still. The world stopped and I wanted to hold this moment forever.

I didn't want anything else of this world.

*

We walked back to the van in a long silent bliss.

'How do you feel?' he asked, piercing the stillness, as we got close to the van.

I looked up at him.

'I actually…' I said, searching for words, 'I actually feel… incredible.'

We laughed.

'Yes,' he said, 'me too.'

All around us the forest was a lush explosion of contrast, light, shadow, texture. And if I listened carefully enough it sounded as though the forest was breathing. It was full of life and abundance. Before we got into the van, we stood outside kissing each other for a while. Then he stopped suddenly and pulled himself back so he could look into my eyes. He smiled, it was clear he was about to say something.

'What?' I asked, smiling back.

'Are you sure you feel incredible?'

'Of course,' I said.

He paused with a mischievous smile fixed on his face. I searched his face for clues and then my confused eyes stared straight into his and I made it clear I had no idea what he was getting at.

'Remember we agreed that we'd do the mescaline only if we were both in a really great place?'

I didn't have to say anything, my eyes and my grin had said enough.

Seeing Trees

The foolish reject what they see, not what they think; the wise reject what they think, not what they see. ~Huang-Po

The day we had chosen for preparing and consuming the mescaline looked like it would be clear and warm. Jack said that was a very good thing, as there'd be quite a lot of sitting around and waiting to do. It was 6am and only just getting light but we wanted to start early.

Jack pulled out an oblong box that, before we'd crossed the border into Canada, he'd hidden in a secret compartment in the side panel of the van. Inside was a cactus wrapped in clear plastic. I'd expected a Peyote cactus, the one I recognised from my childhood in Mexico, those small, flattened bulbous buds with the white and yellow flower on top, but instead it was a San Pedro cactus. Adam had told him that this one was from the Peruvian Andes, from a very good batch.

The San Pedro had lengthy, girthy, ribbed stems, and when Jack cut into one the cross section looked like a star with seven points. He cut off a section around two feet long for the two of us. He said it was enough and that we'd have a little left over if we decided to do it again. He put the remaining bit of cactus back in the box, careful not to prick himself with the spines as he did it. He unfolded some notepaper – the instructions for the preparation from Adam. I sat down, put a rug over my shoulders, and stroked Oak, who had decided to rest her head on my lap. I watched while Jack got out all the things he needed and laid them out on the earth in front of me. A gas canister, camping stove, several large bottles of water, a large cooking pot, two knives, two lemons, a wooden spoon, and a battery powered blender. The blender was also a gift from Adam, Jack told me, solely for the purpose of extracting the mescaline. He kept checking back to his small page of handwritten notes. Then he mumbled something to himself and went round to another part of the van and rummaged through some things. A few moments later he came back round to the back of the van with a cotton t-shirt in his hand and he placed it down with the other objects. He started packing the items in a large empty backpack.

Soon we were carrying the kit deep into the forest. We followed a path for a while and then veered off, wading through fern and shrubs I didn't know the names of. Within about twenty minutes we reached a small clearing and decided it would be our spot. I put my bag down, looked around me. An ocean of foliage surrounded us. I closed my eyes and tried to remember the colour green. I breathed in deeply and I could smell a delicious mixture of decaying bark, fresh greenery and fungi.

Jack unloaded his backpack and arranged the contents onto a large rug he'd spread out onto the uneven ground. We sat down opposite each other with all this stuff between us, and I watched him as he consulted his instructions and proceeded to arrange the objects in a way that made more sense to him.

'What can I help with?' I asked.

He cut the cactus in two, passed one half over to me carefully, and handed me a knife. 'Here, cut this up into slices,' he said.

And so, together, we began to prepare the cactus. He'd warned me that the preparation would take a long time. We cut it up into slices, then into smaller pieces. Then he reached for the blender and put a few handfuls of the cactus pieces in with some water. After blending them he poured the mixture into the cooking pot and then repeated the blending of cactus pieces with water until all the cactus pieces had been used up and the pot was two thirds full of a frothy mixture. Then he put the pot on the gas stove and started heating it.

'Okay,' he said, 'now we have to be patient. This is going to be heating for at least another three hours.'

'Are you serious?'

He nodded.

'Do you think it's safe? What if someone finds us?'

He shrugged and smiled.

'Well,' he said, 'we're already on the run anyway. Being caught for making cactus soup is hardly a big deal considering the circumstances.'

I laughed. He was right. I'd almost forgotten we were running away. And, strangely, now that he'd reminded me, it didn't seem to bother me as much as it perhaps should have. I wasn't overcome with anxiety. Besides, running away was hardly the right term for it anymore. No one was running.

'And anyway,' he said, looking around him at this beautiful secluded secret spot of ours, whilst he stirred the mixture, 'we're not going to get caught.'

*

So we had at least three hours to wait. During the first half hour or so Jack stirred the mixture regularly and checked its consistency. Later on it was left to mostly just simmer by itself.

Jack wanted to make sure it had boiled for long enough, so in the end he left it on the heat for over four hours. He ripped the t-shirt and placed it over the mixer, using it as a strain as he poured over the contents of the pot little by little. Gradually the liquid seeped through the t-shirt into the mixer, and a pulp was slowly left behind. He waited a good while until the pulp had cooled down enough,

wrapped the t-shirt round the pulp completely and then squeezed any remaining liquid out.

'Ta-dah!' he said, pointing to the juice.

'Is that it?'

'Yes.'

'Finally! And what… we just drink it?'

'Yes. Once it's cooled.'

He cut a lemon into quarters. He consulted his piece of paper one last time, and then finally poured the juice out into two cups.

'Okay, here,' he said, passing me a cup. Then, with a grin on his face, he placed a full bottle of water and the lemon quarters between us. 'We'll need these,' he said. 'It's going to taste disgusting.'

How right he was. It was the most disgusting, slimy, bitter thing I had ever tried in my life. Though I'd imagined it would taste bad, I hadn't expected it to be quite as horrible as it was. After just one tiny – barely a – sip, I retched. I rinsed my mouth with water. I sucked on a lemon piece as hard as I could, screwing my face up from the sourness. I glanced over at Jack. He was doing pretty much the same. Then, I counted to three, pinched my nose and gulped that small amount of cactus soup down as quickly as I could. Finally I sucked hard on another piece of lemon, as though I was doing a tequila shot – if only! I wanted to laugh at us both but I felt too nauseous. I got up and walked towards a tree. I leaned against it, doubled over. I was convinced I was about to throw up. But somehow I didn't. I walked back to Jack who looked like he was concentrating on some deep breathing. I sat down next to him, took his hand in mine and smiled, not just at him, but at everything.

*

Green! An explosion of green! I see green, and blue and red and yellow! My god! Colour! Glorious colour! I am so moved, I want to cry.

Oh god! The trees! They're bursting with life. Each insect, each drop of water, and each leaf in this living forest is seen in its raw form: astonishing, beautiful and improbable. A miracle. I am captivated.

Life is vibrating and pulsating all around and within. What is inner and what is outer? I no longer feel the separation between the two.

Direct vision. Immediate life. Total mind-shattering clarity.

All the things I ever learned are suddenly unlearned; all those words and concepts fall away to reveal life as it is, not as I had dreamt it was. All acquired knowledge is replaced by a direct, absolute and intense knowing. Knowing everything, knowing the mystery, without knowing how. No need to ask why.

In a puff of smoke Silvia's story drops away and I stand in front of life. Raw naked life. Delicious and stunning.

I have no hallucinations. Instead I see everything as if for the very first time… and it is all extraordinary. Everything's changed, but in a sense nothing's changed at all. The ordinary has become extraordinary. What was here before is still here, except there is no longer a veil blocking me from seeing it. Actually seeing it. No longer a prism distorting my vision. I finally see the world.

And it is all so clear and simple that I can't help but burst out laughing! It was always so obvious and yet I couldn't see! How ridiculously wonderful, stupidly magnificent!

And everything is light. Beautiful resplendent light.

My mind is empty and I'm just so… relaxed.

*

It was getting dark when we began to pack things up. We hadn't really spoken to each other much, but there was no need for talking. Words seemed unnecessary. We smiled and we knew. We just knew.

We walked back to the van and I relished every sensation, my feet pressing the earth, the plants brushing against my skin, the crunch of branches beneath my feet, the tink tink sound of the metal cup strapped to Jack's backpack that shook with his every step. I couldn't see colour anymore, that only lasted a moment, but I didn't need to. Everything was perfect as it was.

We weren't hungry and we couldn't sleep, so we just lay there in the van for hours holding each other, until the morning sun rose again.

*

As a young child I saw the world for what it was. Every waking moment was filled with awe at the inexplicable magic trick of existence. It's been here ever since, except the difference now is that I have grown used to it. I take it for granted and so I cannot see it. It is hidden behind a veil of normality. A veil of concepts, words, labels and ideas. A veil of perception. I think I know what a tree is, therefore I cannot see the tree.

What can I say of my mescaline experience except that it reminded me of something I'd sensed as a child, and that I'd come close to during my moments of flow whilst painting. What the eye sees when it truly sees… it takes your breath away.

I was still buzzing from the memory of the experience the next morning as I lay by Jack's side waiting for him to wake up. The mescaline had now definitely worn off, and I felt like I wanted to talk again. He stirred and finally opened his eyes.

Jack was amazed to find out that I had seen colour during my trip. We discussed and compared our trips at length and we found ourselves finishing each other's sentences because of the similarities.

We laughed together in a way that we had never laughed before. The laughter of mad men – or perhaps those who have just been cured of their madness. And at other times we were silent. We'd just stare at each other with wide eyes and knowing smiles.

'Jack,' I said at one point, 'remember at the beginning you were worried that the trip might be a disappointment? Well, was it?'

'No, definitely not disappointing.'

'But was it similar to what happened on the beach?'

Jack took a while to reply.

'Similar perhaps, but not the same. In a sense they're incomparable.'

'In what ways?'

'I guess on the beach it was completely unexpected. So the whole thing was more powerful and... absolute.'

'How d'you mean?'

'I don't know Silvia. They're both just memories now though, it doesn't matter what happened and what they were like. The details don't matter. It's this though, isn't it?' he said, his face once again alight with a smile, 'It's right here. It's not about yesterday or Montauk. It's this. Now.'

Then we both began to laugh again because really it was all so absurd and wonderful.

On that July day that I swallowed a bitter cup of San Pedro mescaline extraction, under a canopy of giant cedar and western hemlock, I saw the world with the clarity of a child's eye. How good it felt to have seen the world in this way again. To be reminded. And how easy it would be to forget.

Calm Before The Storm

Before I knew it we'd spent over three weeks on the island. I was learning the art of relaxation from Jack.

It was as though we had totally forgotten why we'd ever started this journey, now we were just carefree travellers. My time on this enchanted island had been a sensuous mix of swimming, sex, eating, walking and watching Jack perfect his bodysurfing skills while I soaked up the sunshine on the shore. I learned to forage. Sunsets, sunrises, moonrises, meteor showers. It was as though time had melted away along with my fears.

But it was finally time to go. I would miss this place. I still felt that somehow, no matter what happened and what came of my life, I would return to this island. I felt it strongly, and that feeling reassured me. But according to Jack there were still so many other places to see. I had grown used to his attitude of treating this journey like an adventure and an excuse to travel. In fact, I had almost started to feel the same way. However, despite all the blissful moments and experiences on the island, there still remained lodged somewhere deep within, a tiny, tiny part of me that held on to my fears. But those next few days in Whistler, I would break free entirely. I'd step out of the Silvia I knew and I'd become a different person.

*

We walked through alpine meadows and open forest. We smiled at and said hello to any passers-by. We saw many animals, including a herd of deer and marmots – we often heard the shrill whistles of these pudgy rodents as they warned other marmots in the area of any potential danger, apparently that's how Whistler got its name. And on the second night I even awoke to watch a bear sniffing around for food remains outside our van.

All in all, we were as good as on vacation. One night, we set up camp by a large lake. While Jack prepared dinner, I took myself over to the shore and sat down. The moon was high and a couple of days off being full. It was casting a bright trail of light on the black surface of the lake. The air was still and there was barely a ripple on the water. Serenity filled the air. I got up and went to the water's edge, bent down and dipped two fingers in. I splashed some water. *Plip plop.* The sound seemed loud amongst the vast silence. I looked back up at the moon. The moon and I; I wondered how many full moons had passed since the day I'd been born. I stood up and strolled along the edge of the lake, careful not to wet my shoes. That night the moonlight was so bright that it didn't feel like night at all. All around me the earth was lit up, as though it was covered in a translucent sheet of silver.

Every now and then I stopped and turned to look at the moon's long silky reflection in the water: a long and thick vertical line of white that ran from the lake's horizon to my feet, widening the closer it got to me. No matter where I went the moon's reflection always followed me, its line of light always ending at my feet. It was like a rope attached to my feet that ran to the horizon. If there had been a whole line of people standing along the length of that shore each one of us would have seen our very own line of light. But if instead, there'd been no one there to see, there would have been no trail of light at all. And though I couldn't quite comprehend it, it struck me that this lake was both totally illuminated and in darkness all at once.

*

I was exhausted. We'd been walking for seven hours straight since the early morning and my feet were sore. The sun was beating down on us and I'd already almost finished my water supply. We reached a deep, clear, beautiful stream. We took a break. Before I could muster up the energy to take my shoes off, Jack was already testing the water with his feet.

'How is it?' I asked.

'Refreshing,' he said, 'it's lovely, not as cold as I expected.'

I joined him. He was right. The water was still and smooth, the current wasn't particularly strong in this part, and it was right in the path of the sun. Jack stripped down to his boxers and then plunged all the way in.

'Ahh,' he sighed, after his head rose back to the surface, 'amazing.'

The sun was shining straight onto his head, making the drops of water on his face and hair shine like diamonds. I stared as his movements emphasised the muscles on his arms and back. God he was beautiful.

'You should come in,' he said.

I hesitated but after a while I decided to join him. I walked in slowly and shivering, with my shoulders at my ears and my arms wrapped around my chest. And as I finally submerged my body I had a strange flashback. I was a little girl, long ago, in a place I didn't know because my mother was always traveling to new places. We were sitting on the green overgrown banks of a river. We must have been very far away from the rest of the world because she went into the water completely naked. She took me in her arms and held me while I splashed about in the water. Then she pointed me downstream and told me to start doing strokes like a frog, whilst still holding me. *Ribbit ribbit*, she said. I remembered her voice and the way that she said it. I must have been only around four years old. I was tiny.

And with this sudden flashback I felt a weight start to press against my chest. It was a weight I hadn't felt for days, weeks even. I wanted it to go away but it was there, growing, reminding me of everything, of why I was running away, why I was even here in this stream all the way up in Canada. I had to stop swimming. I left the water, wrapped my shirt around my shoulders and sat down on the rocks, resentful and angry. This pain, these memories, they were always ready to greet me.

'What's up?' Jack asked.

And I told him. He left the water, dried himself off roughly, grabbed me by the hand and got me to my feet.

'Come,' he said.

I had no idea what he was doing and where he was leading me, but I followed him. We walked upstream.

'Where are we going?' I asked.

'You'll see.'

He pointed at some flowers I hadn't seen before. He commented on the song of a bird I hadn't noticed. I heard the breeze run through the trees, the low drone of summer insects in the grass, the call of birds near and far and the rocks slip and crunch beneath our feet. The smell of wildflowers flooded my nostrils and the blackness started to drift away.

We carried on walking upstream for another minute or so, when Jack suddenly climbed up some rock cliffs above the stream.

'What the fuck are you doing Jack?'

But I followed him. He took me gently by the shoulders and turned my body around so I was facing downstream, out across the valley.

'Looks pretty from up here, doesn't it?' he said.

It did. Of course it did. The view from this height emphasised the magnitude and beauty of the place even more.

'So what were you saying about your mom?' he said.

'Is that why you brought me up here? To ask me about that?'

'Well, I just thought it'd be easier to talk about stuff up here,' he said.

I was silent. I closed my eyes and breathed the alpine air deeply into my lungs. I felt my skin tingle as drops of water evaporated from it under the sun. I sensed the sun's bright light through my closed eyes and without turning to him I sighed and smiled.

'It doesn't matter.'

We stood there for a while, in silence, looking out from our viewing spot, with only the sound of each other's breath between us, and the slow soothing flow of the stream a few metres below us.

'Are you sure?' he asked.

I nodded.

He put his arm around me, looked down at me and smiled. And although I no longer needed to, I felt reassured. But his caring smile quickly turned into a mischievous grin and, before I got a chance to ask him why, he jumped.

'Oh my god!' I looked down and when I saw his face emerging from the water and smiling up at me I didn't know whether to laugh or to shout at him. 'Fuck Jack, that fucking scared me. You idiot!'

'*That*,' he said, '*that* is why I took you up here! Do it!'

I stared down at him for a few more seconds.

'Fuck!' I said, 'fuck it!!'

And although I'd never done anything like that before, without thought and without fear, I jumped. I fell those few metres through the air and hit the water like a bullet. I opened my eyes before rising and a wash of white bubbles danced around my face. I think even under the water, whilst holding my breath, I was grinning. I surfaced, breathed in and yelled with excitement. I felt invincible.

'Amazing,' I said.

Oak had followed us and was now barking at us from the lower bank. I motioned for her to join us but she didn't even attempt to venture in by herself. I dove under as far as I could with my eyes open. Under the water, with that strange silence in which sounds are warped, it felt like a different world. I kept dipping in and out of that world, rising up and diving down, until I didn't know which world I belonged to.

Later, when the stream had taken us back towards our clothes and our packs, I climbed out and coaxed Oak into the shallows, splashing her fur gently at first to ease her in. She was reluctant, but after a lot of coaxing she was doggy paddling around with us in the deeper parts, under our watchful and protective eyes.

I melted into the moment.

'Jack,' I said, 'I want to go to Alaska.'

And so it was decided. I was determined to see more of this beautiful world, and not knowing what the future held no longer scared me. After that one decisive and fearless jump I'd made into the stream, I was now ready to dive further into the unknown.

All we had to do now was figure out how we would take Oak across the border. Because, we'd decided, she had to come with us. It turned out that hiding a small dog would be much harder than hiding a human. But we still had time to think things through.

*

On our last evening in Whistler as we passed by families, couples and lone travellers sitting at dinner tables I salivated as wafts of delicious food met my nose. I turned to him and said,

'Let's eat out tonight.'

He let out a laugh, but didn't say anything. We'd been very careful with our money so far, not knowing how long it would need to last.

'It's our last day here,' I said, 'let's just allow ourselves this one last treat, ok? Come on, we've had such an amazing time, right? It's on me.'

He turned to look at a couple eating oysters by candlelight, and then at a family devouring three large pizzas between them.

'Okay,' he said, 'yes.'

It took us a while to decide on a restaurant, hovering from menu to menu. Despite our decision to splash out, we knew we couldn't be too excessive. We settled on a lively but welcoming Italian joint that would allow Oak to come and sit under our table as long as she was well behaved. The place was bathed in the light of candles and oil lamps. I imagined the warm golden glow. The smell of fresh garlic, olive oil and baking dough made my mouth water. It was teeming with people but we managed to find a table for two tucked away in a quiet corner and we felt pretty cosy there. I guess it was our first proper date. I didn't mention that to Jack and kept the thought to myself, but I couldn't help but feel excited by it. I wondered what kind of questions I'd ask him if this really was our first date, the first time we were meeting each other properly, and if I was a normal person with nothing to hide. *Impossible,* I thought, *if I was normal, we'd have never met. Fuck normal.*

A waiter came to take our order and we decided on a bottle of red wine and a large goat's cheese pizza to share. The thought of it made me drool. I excused myself and went to the bathroom. I didn't have anything on me, no hairbrush, no make-up and no pretty clothes, just the same frumpy gear I had worn hiking that day, but I tried to arrange myself somewhat. I let down my hair and ran my fingers through it. I bit my lips to let the blood run to them and I pinched my cheeks so that they would get even more colour in them. I noticed for the first time what a healthy glow my skin had acquired from all the hiking in the fresh air and sunshine. I ran a wet finger along my eyelashes and my eyebrows and I rinsed out my mouth. I unbuttoned the first top buttons of my shirt to uncover my chest more. Then I thought that was far too obvious, and I buttoned them up again. I made myself laugh alone in that bathroom in front of the mirror. I stopped and just looked at myself. It had been a while since I'd really just properly stopped to look at myself in a mirror like this.

'Oh Silvia, Silvia, Silvia… look at you… who knew all this would happen?' I whispered, smiling at myself.

It was too much to comprehend. In the last several weeks since leaving San Diego, so much had changed, and here I was now, in an Italian restaurant in the middle of Whistler, British Columbia, an illegal entrant, smiling at myself in a bathroom mirror, while a few metres away, behind a wall, a beautiful man and our beautiful dog waited for me. I could have never predicted any of this. I loved this new story.

I looked deep into my eyes. *Oh Silvia, Silvia, Silvia, who are you?*

*

We sipped on the wine, relishing the taste, as we waited for the pizza to come. We reflected on the day, talked about Alaska, food, Oak, mountains and waterfalls. We toasted our glasses and somehow, we simultaneously managed to blurt out 'to us'. My heart stopped for just a second and a tiny moment of fleeting awkwardness ensued, in which I think I blushed, but that soon passed as we tucked into our delicious meal. We didn't talk about our past. We were consumed by the present.

*

That night I felt warm and glowing, and merry after the wine. We stopped off at a shop and bought a couple of five-litre bottles of mineral water for the journey that was ahead of us. The last few days of hiking and sunshine had left us craving more water than usual. When we turned a corner after leaving the shop I saw Jack pull out a small dark elegant box of *Victoria* chocolates from the sleeve of his jacket.

'Would you like one?' he said, opening the box and grinning over at me.

'How did you—?'

'Well, you know, in my experience there's nothing quite like letting a delicious *Victoria Deluxe* truffle melt on your tongue… their luxury chocolates are divine,' he grinned, putting on a posh accent, 'but they do cost a fortune, and I think we've spent enough money as it is today, don't you?' I looked at him, my face of disbelief slowly subsiding into a smile. 'Besides,' he said, squinting to read the back of the box, 'they're made by *Agra Kraft*. Who on earth would want to give money to a corporation like that? With their track record.' He turned to me once again. 'Perhaps a hazelnut praline truffle,' he continued, '...or a salted caramel?' Finally I burst out laughing, grabbed a chocolate, and put it in my mouth. Butterscotch walnut. God, they really were good. It didn't take us long to empty the contents of that stolen box of chocolates. And as we walked back to the van a few drops of rain fell from the sky and the air felt electric.

While we lay in the van that night, with our bellies full, a huge and powerful storm passed over us. Every now and then Oak would howl and we had to comfort her, until finally she fell asleep, curled up in the passenger footwell.

The sex that night was unforgettable... the sound of the rain, wind and thunder, the smell of the air and earth, the whole atmosphere of the storm made it feel otherworldly. We drifted off to sleep in each other's arms, with Jack still inside me. During that last night in the Whistler area I awoke a few times and felt how the storm shook the van. The rain pelted down onto the metal and the sound was hypnotic. The rumbling thunder reached somewhere deep within me and resonated with my whole being. It spoke to my very core.

A Few Minutes

The next day we were on the road again. The sun was back out as if the storm had just been a dream, but the wet earth confirmed to us that it hadn't been. We left late morning after breakfast, and we drove for hours. We stopped only to refuel and freshen up at a gas station. I was in a delicious daze, watching the views go by outside. It was like a trance. I'd taken it upon myself to make sandwiches for the journey that morning, so that we'd be able to just keep heading north for as long as we could. We drove on and on, mile after mile. I didn't pay attention to signs. I didn't know where we were, and it didn't matter.

In the early evening Jack turned off somewhere and followed a number of smaller roads for some time. Within no more than half an hour we reached a place that felt like it was in the middle of nowhere. Totally isolated from any signs of civilisation. Through a vast, wild, forested valley a wide river carved its way through rock. The sun hit the water and made it glimmer. Jack said the river was the colour of aquamarine.

We went to relieve ourselves in the forest and then we carried the stove, food and a rug upstream to prepare our early dinner. We'd made some last minute extravagant purchases before leaving Whistler, including a bottle of wine, which we drank with our pasta dish. Olives, cheese, sundried tomatoes, pesto and the white chanterelle mushrooms Jack had found the day before. We sat on the plateau of rock and listened to the river. I opened a can of dog food and served it up for Oak. She devoured it, then curled her little body up into a ball, nuzzled herself into a dip in the rock and fell asleep. To finish our meal off, Jack went to collect some water from the stream and we boiled it on the stove and made hot chocolate.

The wine had made me sleepy and I drifted off into a blissful doze, with the evening sun shining on my face and warming my body. I woke up with a shiver. The temperature had dropped but the sun was still shining. Jack was standing over me and smiling.

'I'll take all this back to the van,' he said.

We wrapped and packed everything up and together we carried it back.

We sat in the front seats. We were like two zombies after the food, the wine and the long drive, but it felt good. I wanted nothing more than to curl up with him now, arms around each other, his body heat… but he was determined to go for a swim before the sun set. I pouted as he pulled on his wetsuit. And finally I asked him what I wanted to know.

'Jack,' I said, 'why did you come here?'

'Because we're going swimming,' he laughed. I shook my head.

'No. I mean, why did you decide to up and leave with me in the first place?'

He was silent for a while, looking out at the valley through the windscreen.

'Really,' I said, now looking out at the valley too, 'why? Why did you do it?'

'Well, like I told you, your case is important to me,' he paused. 'And when things suddenly got so weird… we had to leave. You know that.'

'Yes. Of course. I know all that. But, I mean, surely there was something else… you know… another reason?'

'I suppose,' he said and he paused and hesitated a bit before continuing, 'I've always wanted to do this trip. I'd always wanted to go to Alaska with Isabelle. But you already know that.'

I nodded. What I was getting at now, however, was something completely different.

'Yeah, I know that. But it wasn't just that, was it?'

'Probably not.'

'You know, for me, it's like I agreed to come here with you before we even officially had to. That time when you first said *hit the road* it's like in my mind I was already on the road. Maybe,' I paused, 'maybe I was even already decided about it all before that, when I first decided you'd be the person I'd tell everything.'

I stopped. Perhaps it was the wine talking.

'I… I'm sorry, I don't know why I'm saying all of this… I don't even know exactly what I'm trying to say.'

He was nodding. 'I know,' he said, 'it's fine, I know.'

'The point is Jack, I think I'd finally come to realise I had nothing to lose. Nothing. That's why I decided long ago that I was leaving. I just couldn't live like that anymore… so something had to change. And it's like the decision wasn't even mine. It all just happened.'

'I know,' he said, still nodding.

'I realised that the only thing I'd lose was a life that didn't feel mine anyway. And the only thing that felt right at the time was to do something that maybe seemed insane. And that's why I packed my bags when you told me to, without hesitation. That's why I'm here talking shit to you now,' I laughed.

He laughed too. 'No. I know all that,' he said.

Yes, it was true, we'd been through this stuff before.

'Yeah. No. Of course you do,' I said. There was silence again as we both carried on staring at the world outside. Then I half laughed and half sighed. 'I guess,' I said, 'my point right now is that I decided to tell *you* everything.'

'Yes,' he said, 'and I wanted to do this trip with you even before

I knew we'd ever have to.'

My heart started beating faster.

'Hmm…' he said, with mock awkwardness.

'Yeah, hmm…'

We laughed.

'So…' he looked at me, shaking his head and grinning. Then he made to get out the van, 'are you coming for a swim?'

I was far too comfortable in the warmth of my dry clothes. I looked at him, pretending to be pissed off because he was so clearly avoiding the continuation of The Conversation.

'What?' he said, smirking.

'Say it.'

'Say what?'

'Just say it!' I laughed, shaking my head.

'I don't know what you're talking about…'

'You fucking liar.'

My jaw was starting to hurt from all this stupid grinning. I was totally sure he knew what I was getting at.

'Jack!' I said, trying so hard to keep a straight face.

He slid out the door.

'Sorry, what was that?' he said peering in, joking that he hadn't heard me, and immediately he slammed the door so I didn't have a chance to reply. I could see him laughing to himself as he made his way to the front of the van. He looked back at me and waved for me to come out and follow him to the river. I looked back at him still grinning and shaking my head. I got out the van.

'You little shit!' I shouted after him, 'You fucking little immature teenage boy!'

I chased him down towards the water, Oak following us both and barking.

He reached the water's edge and started climbing down some step-like bits that had formed in the rock.

He touched the water with his toes.

'Woah, it's freezing,' he said, turning round to look at me.

'You're insane!' I shouted back.

'You not coming in?'

'No way! Fuck off! You know I'm not!'

'Okay fine,' he said, 'I still like you though,' he said, and for some reason his own words set him off into more fits of hysterical laughter.

'You're such a fucking kid!'

He stood there, smiling down at the water, with only his toes dipped in it.

'I like you a lot!' he carried on shouting, 'I like you Silvia! I like you a lot! I love you! Oh no!' he covered his mouth and looked at me, mock surprise in his laughing eyes. 'Oh no! Oh my god, what have I said?! Ha! I totally just said I love you! I must be out of my mind! I love you! There. I just said it again!'

Before I gave myself time to think anymore, I shouted back at him. 'Fuck you! I love you too. I fucking love you!'

We were laughing like hyenas. Oak was barking like a maniac. Finally he dove in and he roared from the cold. It made me shiver just looking at him. He swam upriver and then down, with a look of delight on his face.

'You're going to freeze you fucking idiot!'

He gave a loud roar and dove under the water. Show off, I thought. I just wanted him to hurry up and get out so I could kiss him. I sat down on a patch of grass between some rocks and then lay back. I looked up at the sky and I smiled uncontrollably. Fuck it. I did love him. If I was a blind idiot, I didn't care.

I fucking loved him. Who knew I would ever come to say those words to someone?

I lay on the warm ground for a few minutes dozing, until Oak's repetitive barking shook me awake. I sat up and looked out to the water, expecting to see a little head bobbing up and down somewhere along the length of the river. But I didn't. I got up and walked closer towards the river. He wasn't there. *Little shit*, I thought, *he's come back in without even telling me. Oh ha ha.* I turned round and walked towards the van to get a better view of it. I couldn't see him. Oak's barking was getting more agitated and she was running up and down the water's edge. I looked back out at the water, scanning far off parts Jack might have drifted to if the current had been particularly strong and he'd decided to swim downriver with it. Oak's barking was driving me insane.

I scanned the water, the banks and the valley. Nothing.

'Jack!' I started shouting.

I shouted towards the forest behind the van.

'JACK?' I shouted louder.

Suddenly I felt like a fool, my voice sounded so stupid and full of anxiety. Of course he was somewhere here. He'd only gone into the water a few minutes before.

'Jack, this better not be a joke! It isn't funny!'

I stood still for a while and looked out towards the water again, silently.

Oh god. Oh god. Jack. Oh god. Where are you? I was running back and forth along the water now, tears blurring my eyes, my legs feeling numb, slipping every few seconds on the jagged banks. No time to think. No point in thinking. All my fears and worries about the authorities were totally void right now. It was getting dark and I wasn't going to find him on my own.

I grabbed my phone from the van and started dialling 911 as I ran back to the water's edge, and just then I stepped too quickly on a loose rock. My ankle suddenly felt like it was on fire. I howled from the pain. I lost balance, and my phone flew out of my hand, shattering to pieces as it bounced off the rock before it hit the water. I grabbed hold of whatever I could so as not to slip down with it. My hands scraped on gravel and then clung to a large sharp rock. I saw blood trickle down the rock before I even felt the pain. And then, through my tears of fear and pain I could barely see a thing. I felt my way back up but soon realised I couldn't stand on my right foot. I used every other part of my body to get back to the van as fast as I could. I needed to find Jack's phone. Oak was running around me, but she couldn't offer any help. I limped my way back, clinging to what I could with my bleeding hands. And when I got to the flatter part and there was nothing left to cling to, I crawled.

I searched through the front and the back, in Jack's bags and boxes, spilling everything out of the van onto the earth, staining things with blood and ignoring the pain in my hands and my ankle, until I finally found his phone. I tried to switch it on. But in vain. The battery was flat and I had no way of charging it.

I climbed my way into the drivers seat. I don't know what I was thinking. I knew it was impossible, but I had to try. Yes, impossible, despite the adrenaline and the determination the pain in my ankle was too real for me to drive. I had nowhere to go, no one to call, I was utterly hopelessly horrifyingly alone.

'Jaaaack! Jaaack!' I started screaming again, over and over, even though I knew it was pointless.

'Where are you Jack?' I cried to myself. 'Where are you? Please Jack. Please. Please come back. Please!'

It was already dark when I returned to the spot where I'd last seen him. That's where I found Oak. She was by the water and howling like a wolf. My body was shaking uncontrollably. I kneeled at her side, held her, and I wept.

*

Later I remembered the radio. The damned radio. I found a local station and let it play forever. Then, in the early hours, a body. *Found by some walkers. A young man, tall, early thirties. Patagonia wetsuit. Likely to have underestimated the strength of the undercurrents. Police are not treating as suspicious.* The next few days passed by in a blur.

Empty Belly

I sat cross-legged in the back of the van, with an open can of sardines cradled in my hands. Eating seemed pointless.

I would sometimes slip into a half sleep, and then I'd suddenly snap out of it and realise.

It now felt like everything that had happened since meeting him had lead up… to this surreal event. Like it was a film I was in, where this outcome had been coming… predestined. As though I'd only ever met him because this was going to happen. His death. He had become his death to me. How could I have ever foreseen any of this? Every time I thought *Jack's dead* I'd shake my head. It became my body's instant reaction to that thought. I didn't get it. He couldn't be.

It had been five days since Jack had disappeared and I was still here, by the river. My hands had started to heal but my ankle was still too sore to drive. I was pretty sure something was broken. I was starving. I was trying to force myself to eat something. Since Jack's disappearance my body had shut down completely and I was sick. Mentally and physically sick. I was faint, drained, tired, nauseous and often delirious. My body had rejected any food I'd attempted to feed it with.

Oak was lying by my side, with her head resting on my lap. I had neglected her these last few days. She had sad eyes. I'd often stared into her big shiny dark eyes and wondered what it was like to be her – to simply lie down in the sun and enjoy it. Simple, instead of having a mind full of incessant thoughts that continually pulled you away from the reality of the moment. I wanted to be free of those thoughts now. I wanted to switch my mind off for a while, to lose my mind.

I lay a hand on Oak's back. She looked up at me without moving and she sighed, and then she readjusted herself, burrowing her head deeper into my lap. Her warmth was soothing. She was delicate with me, as if she knew I was injured.

I looked around at the contents of the van. Jack's clothes were still strewn all over it. A pair of his jeans lay crumpled behind the passenger seat. A pair of his socks lay amongst a batch of canned food near the boot. I put on one of my jumpers and found a hair of his on it. I was surrounded by the memory of him, he was still so real and so present, and yet he wasn't.

My eyes caught sight of the black chiffon shirt I had worn the night we danced at *The Shack*. It was lying under one of his T-shirts. I reached over to pick them both up. I brought them to my nose, breathing in deeply. Oak nuzzled my neck and face, as though she was trying to console me. But it just made me cry even more.

I hugged her and cried into her furry neck.

'Oak... Oak... Oak...' I said, my voice trembling.

I felt such love for her. She allowed me to cry into her and find comfort in her until the sun had lowered itself in the sky and was shining in directly through the windows. Every now and then she readjusted her paw on my lap, as if to remind me that it was there, and that she was there for me. When the tears finally stopped, I pulled away, looked into her eyes and thanked her, stroking her as I did so. I leaned back against the wall of the van again, trying hard to look at it with fresh eyes and without attaching any emotion to any of it. I saw Jack's box of files and documents. My story in a box; the unfinished case.

The Death of Stars

How did he die? What was he feeling? What were his last thoughts? Did he try to get my attention in any way while I lay there on the grass, completely oblivious and wrapped up in my own world? What was the last thing he saw before he took his final breath? I thought back to the things we'd talked about, our discussions on life and death, and I wondered whether his very last moments were ones of total anguish, or if perhaps it was possible that they'd been ones of peace. Perhaps I was deluding myself, but I wanted so much to believe that he hadn't suffered in those last moments. Imagining his torment was too painful.

Jack was dead. I wanted to touch his face, feel the warmth of his body against mine, hear him laugh. He was gone. I closed my eyes and gave myself over to the tears, wishing that I would never have to open those eyes again. Wishing that I could leave this world for good, wishing it wasn't real, wishing it was all a dream. Jack was dead. With my eyes closed I thought that perhaps if I never opened them again this would all disappear and I would never have to confront this nightmare again. I could cry my way to oblivion. Jack was dead.

Painful thoughts drowned me and I didn't have the strength or desire to fight against them. I wanted to disappear. Life was a sick joke. It had been so from day one. Why not have the last laugh and end it all? I'd never have to confront this pain again.

*

I woke from a nightmare. I was cold and needed to pee. I dragged myself out of the van. Oak followed me. I felt so safe with her, and I wondered what I would have been like without her during this last week. It was cold outside. It was dark. I didn't walk far to relieve myself; I was still limping. Before climbing back into the van, I stopped for a moment. I leaned my body weight against the van and I looked up. A myriad of stars glowed above me. Here I was, a small insignificant human being looking up at these balls of fire that were apparently billions of light years away, and that perhaps no longer even existed. It was all so utterly incomprehensible. This vastness. This 'existence' thing.

The night was crisp and the air, though cold, felt fresh on my skin. Oak pressed her silky body against my left leg, supporting her body on mine. She turned her head suddenly as we both heard an owl hooting somewhere not far off. I listened. Frogs were croaking. A soft breeze was whispering through the higher branches of the trees. I looked up and saw their silhouettes sway against the starry sky. In the distance I heard the song of some kind of small bird. The forest was alive, quietly so, and for a brief moment its soothing presence allowed me to forget everything. To forget myself. For a moment, as I stood there, I was simply there, breathing in the presence of the universe, breathing in the presence of a miracle.

I stared up at the sky for a few more minutes, absorbed in its vastness. The music of the forest played in the background as I gazed. My head was empty of thoughts for the first time in days. Oak shifted her body and I realised how cold it was. We got back into the van. I wrapped two blankets around us, cried and we drifted off to sleep.

For the first time since Jack's disappearance, I don't know how, but my dreams were peaceful.

Running From Ghosts

The day I had left my apartment to run away, I had picked up a letter without knowing it. It had concealed itself among the other post – a mixture of junk mail and bank statements. In my rush to escape that day the handwritten 'Silvia de la Luz' didn't catch my eye.

I'd regained some of my senses – it must have been about a week since Jack vanished – I'd made up a makeshift splint for my ankle and started sorting through the van, preparing to leave the wilderness and head back to some kind of civilisation. It was then that I discovered my unopened post, and amongst it this letter:

Silvia,

This is not an easy letter to write but it's time it was written. It's very hard for me to know how to begin this...

Your parents were killed seventeen years ago. My ex-colleague and I were paid to execute them.

You were told a lie about their death. They were killed because of your mother's involvement in the movement against the destruction of the forest near your home by Anders Oil Ltd. This is of course contrary to the official story you received about your father's involvement in a local drug cartel. We had no reason to believe that your father formed any significant part of any cartel.

I am sorry. Very sorry. No words could possibly express my remorse, and I don't imagine they could make much difference to you. If you want me dead, I don't blame you.

I don't know how much you remember from that night. I remember it well. I had never been a man of hesitation. It was not possible in my job. Once a decision was made there was no choice but to carry out orders. But all this changed the night of your parents' death.

My colleague was about to shoot you, but I stopped him. Silvia, you reminded me so much of my own daughter that I couldn't let him do it.

My daughter died eight years ago, and everything changed. I became a different person. When she died I started thinking of you again. To me, you became her.

One night I dreamt about you vividly. It was that night, after endless years of oblivion, that my conscience crept up on me and changed my life. I had to run away of course, mine was not a job you can just retire from. But before leaving that life I felt I had to, in some way, take care of you. Protect you.

I couldn't give you your parents back but I could see to your financial security. The money you thought you were receiving from the Cruz family is from me. Having put everything within my means in place for you, four months later I dropped everything – my wife, my house, my career – and ran away. They haven't found me yet, I was always good at going undercover. They've had a tough time looking for me, but I know they are still searching.

I'm growing tired of running away. I long to be a whole person, but I don't think that's my fate. I am a nobody now. Perhaps tomorrow they'll find me. Perhaps soon I'll be dead. But I am determined to stick it out for as long as I can.

Before writing you this letter I approached you in a café. I hope I didn't scare you, but I'd had a deep desire to talk to you in person for a long time. It's better that you ran off when you did. Perhaps telling you any of this in person would be insanity, perhaps suicide. I'll leave this letter with you tomorrow morning – if you want to talk to me face to face I will knock on your door at 10am. If you choose not to answer I understand.

I live with the most profound regret every day of my life. I know this will not bring your parents back or take away years of pain. I know that none of my words or actions could possibly change a thing.

From the core of my being I am eternally sorry, and I thank you Silvia for making me a changed man.

Juan Ignacio Ruiz

I put the letter down on my lap and burst into hysterical laughter. I imagined showing Jack the letter. He'd put his arm around me. I could feel him doing it, I could smell his skin. He'd tell me it was all the evidence he ever needed for the case. I could hear his voice. We'd continue onto Alaska, but without any of the fear or hiding. We'd be happy. It would be so beautiful. He'd always wanted to go to Alaska. We'd never had to run away.

*

Though this letter had apparently been the missing piece of the puzzle called my life, now, more than ever, nothing made sense. If that man had never knocked on my door and shouted out my name, none of this would have happened. Jack would be alive.

He killed us.

But we'd always both known deep down that we weren't just running away because we thought we had to, but because we both wanted to.

The Plan

I woke up with the light streaming through the windows. For a moment, with my eyes still closed and with the warmth of the sun on my cheeks I felt peace. But only a few moments later I remembered who I was, my story and Jack. Though I would have liked to have had the power to not succumb to these painful thoughts, they gripped me and I found it hard to move. Everything seemed pointless. Getting up was pointless. Moving was pointless. Eating was pointless. Living was pointless. I lay there with the weight of Jack's death pressing me down and making me feel frozen.

Finally I sat up. My stomach rumbled and I was determined to eat. Today I would. If there was one goal for today it was to eat. One step at a time, piece by piece, I could at least try to be a functioning human being again. Though that too seemed pointless. What did it even mean to be a fully functioning human being? Why try to be normal? What point was there in being normal again? It felt ignorant to strive for a more normal and stable state of mind or emotion. Why should I search for the comfort of ignorance? It felt selfish.

Shut up, I said to these thoughts. I needed to eat. My body was surely more intelligent than my mind right now. I would eat, and think nothing more of it.

I searched through the cans, scanning each label and hoping I would find a rice pudding still amongst them. It was the only thing I had a slight appetite for. The beans, the fish, they all repulsed me. After a while of rummaging through the endless mess I found a rice pudding. I took it out, along with a can of sardines for Oak, and I went and sat back down. I opened the can of rice pudding, I ate and I finished the whole thing. It seemed delicious, better than I had expected. I was hungrier than I had realised. Before I knew it I was chewing on the fish as well. I was ravenous. I finished the whole can.

The practical part of me had returned. My body felt stronger, and with it, my mind did too. I opened the door and slid out of the van. The pain in my ankle was finally subsiding, although it was still hugely swollen. I looked up at the sky. Morning dew rubbed against my bare feet. I breathed in the fresh damp air and the smell of fir and I stretched, I felt the need for it. Oak joined me. I looked at her. *It's just you and me Oak.* Today I couldn't let that thought bother me. Today I needed strength from it. I needed strength to figure out a plan. Some kind of plan, any plan.

And I needed to feed Oak. I went to the boot, rummaged through the boxes and found her some food. The mess of cans and boxes made the boot hard to shut. I tried my best to rearrange it all, but cans kept rolling out of nowhere. I tried shoving the boxes further in and jamming loose cans between them to temporarily hold them in. I was struggling and getting irritated. And in this absurd feat of humdrum human existence the box of Jack's documents suddenly fell out and onto the ground. The files and pages exploded out and loose bits of paper started flying off in the wind. I limped after them, grabbing at the air and trying to retrieve each one as fast as I could. I managed to recover them all and place everything neatly back in the box within a minute. But it was only when I was scampering around and grabbing each one so urgently that I realised how important these pages were. How important the contents of this box would be. This box *was* my future plan.

I sat down in a sunny spot outside the van, leaning against it. With the box by my side, my body shielding it from potential gusts of winds, I pulled out one of the files, gripping it tight in my hands. I opened it up and I scanned the words, page by page. A lot of it was incomprehensible, written in English but in a way that made little sense to me.

I carried on looking through the contents of the box, determined, as though I knew what I was looking for. I reached down to the bottom and pulled out what looked like a small notebook. It was a passport. I opened it up. James Alan Harris. Presumably this was Jack's fake passport. Who was James Alan Harris? Why did Jack have this fake passport and how did he get it?

Who was this man who'd briefly crept into my life and consumed it so completely?

I slumped all my weight into the side of the van, I sighed and I looked out into the space in front of my eyes, as if searching for inspiration. And suddenly I knew what I had to do with all of this. I knew what I had to do with my unfinished case and all my questions.

What was his name? Jack's lawyer friend, the one who gave him the mescaline? He'd mentioned him so many times… Adam! I rummaged through the box, looking for Jack's little black notebook, where he kept his list of contacts. It wasn't in there. I got up and went round to the front of the van. I checked the glove compartment and the floor under the driver's seat, and finally I found the notebook in the left car door compartment, jammed between a copy of *The Milepost: Alaska Travel Planner* and a guidebook on edible mushrooms.

I felt I was onto something. I felt determined. I opened the notebook and flicked through it, scanning each page until I got to the part with contacts. I searched for Adam's name. Then I searched again, even more carefully. He wasn't there. But there was one address on a separate page, which had no name. I knew San Diego well enough, I recognised the address as being near the Horton Plaza mall where we'd started the journey. I remembered Jack had said that Adam lived very near there. I remembered he'd told me that Adam was the only person he knew who lived so close. This had to be Adam's address and number. I was sure of it. Suddenly I was overcome with a strange sense of relief.

This story wasn't over, I was taking it to Adam.

But first, I would go to Alaska.

Closure

I had spent a whole two weeks in that place. The van stayed put.
I had been waiting for my ankle to heal. And all that time there
was an imaginary hope, a lingering pathetic hope that somehow he
would still miraculously turn up. Of course he would. Jack wasn't
gone. No way. That wasn't possible. No. He would appear. Any
minute he'd be back.

On the fourteenth day I sat down where I had once told Jack I
loved him. How all-consuming yet fleeting that moment had been.
Sitting in that spot now I looked out across the valley. I sat and
stared for hours with Oak resting by my side. The sun kept us warm.

Sometime in the afternoon, I found a closure of some kind.
I was watching the sky and remembering the colour blue when I
noticed a dark dot flying high up there. As it grew I saw that this
dot was in fact a large bald eagle, soaring in my direction. I thought
perhaps it was going to swoop down to catch a fish from the water,
but it missed the river and was clearly heading towards us. I grabbed
Oak out of fear, to protect her. The bird landed only a few metres
away, as though it was totally oblivious to mine and Oak's presence. I
was utterly stunned. I had never been so close to one of these birds.
This one must have been a female because it was so big, possibly
over a metre in length. She perched herself there on those rocks and

197

looked out at the valley with us. Unmoving, like a statue, though she clearly knew that we were there. And what seemed even stranger was that Oak had also noticed the bird, yet she hadn't reacted either. I sat there motionless, holding my breath and in awe of what I was witnessing. It was unreal. This beautiful vision had managed to snap me out of my paralysis.

Suddenly I was overcome with a sense of peace. I found it symbolic in a way I couldn't quite fathom. *Energy never dies,* Jack had once said, *it just transforms.* I saw the sheer beauty of that valley and I felt comfort in knowing that Jack was now totally immersed in that world. He died doing what he loved. *Energy never dies.* It didn't make the pain of losing him go away, but it felt like a goodbye. Whatever all this was, for me it was closure.

Adam

Reaching Alaska had given me some kind of purpose and an unexpected sense of hope. Strangely it felt like the right thing to do, even though I knew there were no right or wrong decisions to be made, there were only decisions. Jack wasn't with me, but he was the reason I was going, and I still felt we were doing this together. What exactly would I do in Alaska? How long would I stay there?. A few days? Weeks? Months? Years? Who knew? I couldn't see that far into the future.

But those weren't the biggest concerns. After the last week of delirium in which my thoughts had made little sense and I hadn't been able to think straight, I was now finally able to reflect upon my situation with some clarity. And things were far more complicated than I had realised.

How would I get to Alaska? *That* was the problem. How on earth would I cross the border?

According to that letter, border crossings weren't a problem anymore, because I'd never had to run away in the first place. No one was looking for me. I had been running from a ghost. The knowledge of this should have freed me up to go wherever I wanted, without fear. But actually it was perhaps more complicated than that. I had entered Canada illegally. I wasn't supposed to be here. So who knew what might await me at the Alaskan border?

And so I decided that, before I did anything else, I had to get in touch with Adam.

For a long time, a million miles away from clarity and at the depths of sorrow, I hadn't felt any responsibility at all to let anyone know. Jack's friends and family must have been starting to wonder where he had disappeared to. From the list of Jack's contacts, Adam would be the only one I could explain everything to and ask advice from. He was the only one I imagined could possibly understand anything about me, and what had happened. It would have to be his responsibility to tell the others. I couldn't possibly do that.

So, finally, after two weeks of mourning in that valley, I hit the road again. I vowed to myself that even though I didn't know quite where I was, I would have to somehow try to remember this place forever. As I drove I tried to memorise the route, telling myself I would one day return to that place.

*

I used a pay phone to call Adam. I rehearsed my lines a good few times before dialling the number. I would keep the call as brief as I could, let him know that I'd fill him in on the rest when I saw him.

It rang for a long time and then went to voicemail. I tried again. My heart was beating fast. This time, after the fifth ring he picked up.

'Hello?'

I paused, unable to speak quickly enough. I was unsure what to say. I had memorised it all but now the words fell away.

'Is this Adam?' I said.

'Yes. Who is this?'

In a final moment of panic I put the phone down. I would write him a letter. I could say so much more in a letter. I was a coward. I decided I'd write him a detailed letter, send it, give it a week and then call to check if he'd received it. I'd let him know everything in the letter. Then we could talk. And in the meantime I'd start heading north. That's what I decided. And it felt good to have made a decision.

Lost

Attempting to memorise the exact site of Jack's disappearance had turned out to be futile, my mind soon fogged over, so I pulled over and marked out my best guess on a map. Everything seemed to have lost its significance, blurred into one muddled memory. All I knew was that I was heading north. That was enough for now and I didn't feel like I needed or wanted to know much more than that. I wasn't yet ready for complete lucidity.

I checked myself in for two nights in a motel somewhere along the Alaska Highway. I hadn't properly washed myself for days. As I rummaged through the van and pulled out the things I'd need for my stay, I came across the shopping bag with the packet of blonde hair dye. Never used. There was something sinister about it. It was a grotesque reminder of the fact we'd never had to run away.

The middle-aged lady at the desk was friendly, despite the fact I looked a mess and must have smelled terrible. She didn't ask questions, just smiled and told me to enjoy my stay. She even bent down to stroke Oak before showing me to my room.

It was small and simple, but comfortable. A single bed, a small wooden bedside table, a lamp and a guidebook to British Columbia and the Yukon. A chest of drawers, a television, and a small window. I sat down on the bed. It was too springy and soft for my liking; I had grown used to sleeping in the van. I got up, undressed myself and took a shower. The warm water felt incredible. I stayed in the shower for far longer than I needed, allowing myself to indulge in the simple pleasure of feeling warm water stream over my skin. I scrubbed every pore on my body. I washed my hair and spent a whole three minutes brushing my teeth. And then I sat down and let the water pour all over me while I closed my eyes and drifted in and out of what felt like a dreamlike state. Finally, I turned the shower off and dried myself with the towel provided by the motel. It smelled like fresh laundry. I hadn't smelled that scent in a while. I rubbed and rubbed my skin repeatedly, as though I was trying to get rid of some kind of dirt. I hand-washed all of my clothes and hung them up to dry on the pegs on the door and handles on the chest of drawers. I lay naked on the bed and fell immediately into a long, deep sleep.

I woke up feeling healthier than I had in weeks. I used the extra clarity I had gained from the long sleep to formulate the letter to Adam. It took me six hours of frustration, tears and endless revisions. The letter turned out to be a fourteen-page essay in which I told him everything as best I could, asked questions and demanded answers.

I had predicted that writing that letter would be like opening up every wound of my psyche and pouring salt all over each one of them. I wasn't wrong. After everything, all my epiphanies and revelations, after gaining and losing so much, I found myself back on the knife-edge. Darkness eclipsed me. I was lost again.

Jack

From all over the world people came to seek asylum in the US, and of all the nations, the US's southern neighbour had it the worst. Every day, in an attempt to escape violence and persecution, Mexicans arrived at the US border, and only a tiny percentage of these people were let through and granted refugee status. The rest were denied entry, turned away and sent back. Illegal crossings were an option, but an option only open to a few. They were too expensive for most, and too risky for others.

Jack Rhodes and Adam Harding used to go to Mexico together regularly when they were at university. Adam was a surfer and he went there for the waves, and Jack came along to try to perfect his bodysurfing skills. With Adam's boards strapped to the roof of Jack's van, and the inside of the vehicle a total mess, with tents, sleeping bags, towels, sunscreen, surf wax and all sorts of paraphernalia strewn across every inner part of the van, the two friends ventured south as often as they could. They were young and single and the endless hours spent in the water were punctuated only with parties, tequila and overindulging in Mexican food. A total escape from their studies and everything they identified with back in San Diego.

Sometimes they even just broke free for short weekend trips across the border, going not much further than Ensenada, but often they went for longer, and much further. They had been to Mazatlán a few times before. Adam had met a girl there. There were a variety of surf spots for Adam to choose from, and soon enough they'd made a lot of friends, so even after Adam's romance had fizzled out, the two would often make Mazatlán their final destination during a road trip, or stop off there before heading further south if they had more time.

During one of those visits, while enjoying a beer after a long session out in the water, Jack and Adam enquired after two of their friends – two brothers, Cristian and Felipe, who had been working at the bar. After a bit of investigation they got news of the fact that the two brothers and their family were in hiding after having been witnesses to a cartel crime. They had been denied asylum by the US and didn't have enough money to afford the illegal means of crossing the border that had been offered to them. The full story was horrifying, and Jack and Adam spent the rest of that trip discussing the possible options for the two brothers and their family. A plan was devised. Jack and Adam headed back to San Diego to renovate the van, while their Mexican friends went about obtaining fake documents: driver's licences, social security numbers, a license plate and even credit cards. Everything to prove their new identities.

It took a total of three trips over a period of almost two months to transport the two brothers and their family to the US. Straight-faced machine-gunned guards lurked around on the road as you waited in traffic queues at the Mexico-United States border. You avoided eye contact at all costs. Those long queues gave you enough time to stress and panic even if you had nothing to hide. But as usual, Adam and Jack strapped two surfboards to the top of the van, threw towels, board shorts, rash vests and sleeping bags around the van, so as to make it all look as unassuming as possible; just two friends heading out for their usual surf trips. Nothing to be suspicious of. They even made a habit of making sure all the curtains on the windows were open. *We're not hiding anything.*

Once back in the US, Jack and Adam handed the family over to a team of human rights and immigration lawyers. Pete, my model, who Jack had stepped in to cover that first day I'd ever met him, had been an important part of that team. It's funny how much you don't know about people.

The trips changed the two students, making them even more passionate and active in the sphere of politics and human rights. Perhaps they were naïve and reckless to think they could ever get away with it. But they were cunning. Keeping up to date with current affairs, they always timed their crossings with major events or crimes. They chose days when border authorities had their minds fixated on catching the bigger criminals. And so, despite the existence of X-rays and heartbeat detectors, which could have been used at any time, they did it. They outwitted border control. Full of empathy, passion and drive they repeated similar trips over the course of the year that followed, risking their own lives and security. And although they were regularly offered money, or other kinds of compensation, they never took a cent for any of it.

They finally stopped when they got a reality check and lost that feeling of invincibility after a close call with border control. Just over a week after they made their last such border crossing, Jack was in New York visiting his family. And that's when it happened. There on that Montauk beach. On that day. In that moment. The meaning of life changed so suddenly and so absolutely.

Jack had never told me any of this – about the illegal crossings, about the fake IDs, about any of it – just as he had never told anyone. It had remained a secret. I doubt Adam had ever wanted to tell anyone this either, but keeping secrets from me now would have been pointless. After all, I too was no longer a secret to him.

An Explosion of Stars

The evening sun flickered between the silhouettes of the tall trees that lined the highway. Flashes of glowing light caught my eyes and warmed my face as I drove along the long empty road. The beauty only saddened me. That all-consuming sorrow had come back again, it was clinging on hard, and I felt helpless and resigned. There was a big part of me that just wanted to get lost, to give up.

I drove like a robot, my every movement automatic. My body felt drained and empty. This unshakable sadness was threatening to become me. I was a ghost. I closed my eyes and watched as light danced and flickered on the blackness of my eyelids. Helpless and hopeless, I wanted to give up and give myself over. In fact, I felt ready to wake up from this illusion, this nightmare I called my life. I felt ready to die. And the lights, how they danced on my lids, like an explosion of stars...

Oak's violent bark sent a spasm of shock through my body, from my toes to the crown of my head. I opened my eyes, heard a loud honk, saw the lumber truck approaching us fast. I swerved just in time. The truck ground to a halt and I pulled into the grassy verge immediately. I looked back to see the truck driver's angry face peering out of his window. I shot out of the van. I didn't make out what he was saying, in my dizzy state, only heard a jumble of words and a blur of sounds. 'I'm sorry,' I kept repeating, 'I'm so sorry!'

It was on that day, before the sun had set completely, that I finally realised just how much I wanted to live.

Colour

I was still crying from the shock. I was so incredibly grateful to be alive.

In a flash all this would have ended, would have gone. I would have never been able to smell the earth again, to feel this breeze or the sun on my skin again. The sky and the trees would have disappeared. I was so incredibly happy, euphoric, to still have all this. To still be alive.

For ages I walked and walked and walked along the verge, in this enchanted state, marvelling at everything… at life. How magnificent my life now seemed, despite all its flaws, now that I'd so narrowly escaped death. This human experience, with its highs and lows.

I sat down on the verge, still recovering from the shock, and I looked at the forest around me. These trees were tall and ancient, and a gravelly sandy path led into the forest – it was drenched in the evening sun and seemed warm and inviting. Oak sat next to me. My true friend.

Trees. How strange a thing trees were. Tall spikes of wood shooting out from the earth beneath them. Energy growing towards the sky.

Rays of light pierced through the forest. The sight of them took my breath away. I felt their gentle warmth caress me. A deep sense of love suddenly surged through my body: an infinite, all-consuming explosion of love, for everything. So explosive it stunned me and brought tears to my eyes. I heard a flutter of wings to my right, my head turned towards the sound. A group of five swallows rose from a large branch, as though without reason or purpose, for they simply floated and danced in the air above me, back and forth, round and round, up and down, pirouetting and suspended in space.

'Jack,' I whispered into the air, without even realising I had done it until the sound echoed in my ear.

It's like the fish swimming around and wondering what water is and where to find it. When something is so obvious, you can't see it. And it remains hidden from you because you are looking for it. You look for it everywhere and yet it's the very make up of who you are, of everything, of life. Being. Just being. It's closer to you than breathing itself. Life is the treasure.

These words of Jack's suddenly flooded back to me, so clear, as though he were there, speaking them again.

I stretched my arms out towards the big blue open sky as though it was the most natural thing to do. Colour. Breathtaking colour. Gold light glowed through the gaps in my fingers. I smiled like a child. Light. That strange and mysterious thing called light. The prisms dropped away and life, in all its glory, was finally seen. I breathed a sigh of profound relief.

Epilogue

New Life

Seven months later, I sat on the step of the wooden veranda, cradling a cup of coffee in my paint stained hands. Blues, turquoises, emeralds, jades. Navy, silver and gold. I had been painting the sea and stars that day. It was cold out, but I was still glowing with the warmth from indoors. The rug over my shoulders smelled of burnt wood from the fireplace. I loved that smell. Here I was outside my home watching the sunset over Cox Bay once again. Oak lay beside me, resting her head on my lap.

I had made a ritual of this, yet each time I sat there the beauty astounded me. It never faded.

Today as I sat there, pressing the warmth of the cup very gently onto my swollen belly, I thought about that last stormy night in Whistler all those months ago. Our beautiful night of reckless passion. That night was emblazoned in my mind. I smiled. Remembering Jack was not painful any more. Remembering him was remembering what it meant to be alive.

After the last ray disappeared behind the horizon, I got up and walked back into the warmth. I was feeling sleepy, but I wanted to add the final touches to the stars I had been painting on the ceiling that day. Yes, little Philip's room would be my most beautiful work of art yet.

*

Acknowledgements

I thank Valerie Brandes and Jazzmine Breary at Jacaranda Books for believing in my work from the start. You have provided me with such an incredible means for expression, and for that I am truly grateful.

My editor, Lucy Llewellyn, for her excellent work in sculpting this book from a lump of rock to something more akin to (hopefully!) a polished gem. It's been a blast working with you!

All those involved in the completion of this book, including the copyeditor, the proofreader, and friends and family who read and critiqued the book.

My family and friends for their patience and support when I was at times forced to become a social recluse whilst working on this book. I feel so very fortunate to have such great people surrounding me.

My mother, Julita Walczak, for inspiring in me a love of books and all beings. And for, in my final moment of panic and doubt, making me realise that it's totally okay to write a love story.

My father, Marek Walczak, for his enthusiasm and sparks of inspiration when I came into pickles at certain points of the story – especially that one time in Thetford Forest.

Both my parents for igniting in me a love for the outdoors and the natural world. For their continued belief in me and for their support, despite the odds.

My sister, Zosia Walczak, for very probably having been my biggest inspiration to be creative in the first place. For our most recent deep chats about this funny ol' thing called life and the nature of reality and existence, while gazing up at the moon or during long walks, or while dancing like no one's watching in the early hours.

All the libraries and charity shops that have over the years made books more accessible to me.

And finally, life – this weird and wonderful thing – for being the greatest inspirer of them all.